When Babette St. Clair went masked and dressed as a gypsy to the Mardi Gras ball – strictly against her family's wishes – she should have guessed that someone would soon penetrate her disguise. Unfortunately that someone was the debonair ex-riverboat gambler, Grant Tyler; but Grant did not intend to take advantage of the discovery until the passion he felt for Babette turned to hatred, after she left him without a word to marry the ruthless Ralph Weldon.

Grant was not to know that Babette's loveless marriage was in name only, and had come about because of a sinister family secret. He was consumed only with the thought of revenge for her fickleness, and the idea of humiliating her before the whole of fashionable New Orleans society . . .

By the same author in Masquerade

FRANCESCA

Gambler's Prize
Valentina Luellen

MILLS & BOON LIMITED
London . Sydney . Toronto

First published in Great Britain 1969 by Wright & Brown
Ltd., 18 Stukeley Street, London W.C.2.

© Valentina Luellen 1969
This revised edition
© Valentina Luellen 1978
Australian copyright 1978
Philippine copyright 1978

This edition published 1978 by Mills & Boon Limited,
17-19 Foley Street, London W1A 1DR

ISBN 0 263 72847 1

Filmset in 10 on 11pt Plantin

Made and printed in Great Britain by
C. Nicholls & Company Ltd
The Philips Park Press, Manchester

CHAPTER ONE

"LOUIS, you must not go to that awful gambling house again." The girl's soft voice was full of anxiety. "If father should find out he will be terribly angry."

Louis St. Clair swung round to face his sister, a half-full glass of brandy in one hand, and his handsome features broke into a complacent smile.

"Really, my dear, I'm no longer a child. I come and go as I please from this graveyard of a house. You mean well, Babette, but I wish you wouldn't fuss quite so much, it unnerves me. Last night at the tables I was not up to my usual form because of the lecture you gave me."

"Or too much to drink," Babette St. Clair said icily.

Her brother's answer was to finish his drink and turn towards the door. "Louis – wait!" She caught his arm contritely. "My tongue will be the death of me. I did not mean to speak so harshly, but tonight the Mardi Gras begins and you promised to escort me. With Ralph away, I cannot go out alone."

Louis looked down into his sister's large blue eyes and was ashamed. She always made him feel this way after an argument, whether it was his fault or not. Sceptically he allowed his gaze to dwell on her carnival costume.

"Did our illustrious father see your attire before he left for Baton Rouge?"

"Of course not, I hid it. What do you think of it?"

Babette pirouetted before him. After great contemplation she had decided not to be Marie Antoinette or a fashionable lady of the French court, but a gypsy girl – something her father would consider highly unsuitable for the daughter of

an eminent banker. As it was he had conveniently gone away
on business the previous day. The dress she wore was a vivid
shade of red hugging tight to a tiny waist, the neckline
curving low around slim shapely shoulders. The contrast
against softly tanned skin was stunning. Large gold earrings
dangled from her ears and her long black hair was loose –
hanging almost to her waist.

Louis burst unexpectedly into laughter and she frowned
angrily, totally unaware of the seductiveness of her costume.

"Why are you laughing? Don't you like it?"

"It's marvellous, sweet – every man in New Orleans will
want to dance with you."

"Then why – ?"

"Do I laugh?" Louis became serious again. "Because we
are so alike – wanting more from life than our parents have
had. You chide me for gambling and drinking – yet you long
for excitement, to break away from the family chains too.
Why else would you choose such an audacious costume? We
both hate living under the shadow of the St. Clair name –
forbidden by the conceited shroud of respectability to for-
sake tradition. It makes me sick. For a few hours I shall
gamble, probably lose and drink myself into a stupor. The
thought gives me great satisfaction."

"And me?" Babette asked quietly. It was as if he could
read her mind!

"You will be swept along by the carnival spirit – suitably
masked so that no one will recognise the beautiful gypsy girl
dancing in the arms of a young man – held a little closer than
propriety allows. When Mardi Gras is over I shall continue
my wayward habits and you will become the wife of a'
respected humbug. Poor Babette – your future may not
prove to be very exciting so enjoy yourself while you are
able."

Babette was silent. How she wished he had not mentioned
her forthcoming marriage – it made her afraid to step out into
the streets and enjoy herself as Louis wanted. If Ralph, her
fiancé, ever found out –

"Contemplating the consequences?" her brother teased. "Come now – since when have you been afraid of Ralph. He is ten years your senior and inclined to feel your high spirits need taming somewhat, but I do not believe he would take a whip to you."

"I am not afraid," Babette declared resolutely. "To prove it – I am coming with you to Sans Souci; you may play at the tables for a while, then I shall drag you away to have fun with me. It's so long since we had fun together, Louis. Please."

Her entreaty touched his heart as she knew it would. Drawing her to him he planted a kiss on her forehead.

"You win – witch."

Babette's recollection of Sans Souci was of a huge, palatial house slowly falling into ruins. The once splendidly tended gardens no longer cared for, the grounds leading down to the bayou St. Michael, overgrown with weeds – desolate. It had been an old familiar story, not unlike that of the St. Clair family itself, but whereas they retained some dignity and a little money, the owners of Sans Souci had been forced to sell out completely and, disgraced, had left New Orleans. No one had bought the plantation and for years she had ridden in the grounds and picnicked in the shade of the trees along the bayou, completely unchallenged.

Now, as the coach turned into the long driveway leading up to the house she drew in her breath in amazement.

The tall, three-storeyed white house was ablaze with lights. Carriages lined the forecourt, people milled around the entrance, some in carnival attire, others in evening dress, the women weighed down with glittering jewellery. Whether they approved of the newcomer or not, the élite families in New Orleans were not going to miss this opportunity to take a good long look at him, and whisper their speculative gossip behind white-gloved hands, Babette thought.

The french windows which lined the wisteria-covered galleries, were thrown wide open and the hubbub of voices floated down to mingle with the noise of horses and carriages.

It was another world to her! Exciting – challenging – dangerous! Yes, dangerous, for if her identity were ever discovered . . .

For a moment she hesitated as a liveried Negro in dark green opened the carriage door, and Louis climbed down. She knew that her brother would spend little time with her once the gambling tables caught his attention. She could wander freely among the revellers – even place a bet of her own if she chose, but she knew she would never have the courage to act so audaciously.

"Quite a change, eh?" Louis said, helping her to alight. "No more early rides for you."

A Negro boy took their cloaks and gloves and they moved on past masked revellers to the main room. Louis chuckled.

"The place is packed – thanks to Mardi Gras. The wearing of masks is so convenient, *n'est-ce pas*? For three whole days the most respected families in town can gamble to their hearts' content without a stain on the family honour. Come on – let us try our luck."

Babette hung back.

"No, Louis – you go alone. I will just watch."

He shrugged, his face already alight at the prospect of dicing once more with Lady Luck.

"Suit yourself."

Awe-stricken, Babette wandered through the downstairs rooms, mingling unnoticed amid the crowds. She could hardly believe the magnificent splendour before her eyes. Thick, richly coloured carpets and drapes – crystal chandeliers – long mirrors lining the length of some walls. The atmosphere was tense with excitement and her heartbeats quickened. Never before had she so openly defied propriety – moving alone, unchaperoned, unrecognised – free to do as she pleased.

Drawn to the tables she watched the spinning roulette wheel, holding her breath each time it slowed and the croupier called out the winning number, seeing the looks of depression or joy registered on the faces around her.

The room was crowded. Those who were not jostling each other at the tables stood around in groups, talking – or admiring the elaborate décor of the rooms. Impassive-faced Negroes in their green livery came and went with trays of ice-cold champagne, which Babette noticed seemed to be in endless supply. She took a glass and stood to one side, content just to watch and listen. There were many faces she recognised – the bank manager, business friends of her father's. Were the women with them their wives or mistresses, she wondered? Who could tell when they were masked? The vivacious young dark-haired girl with old Claud Abelard was certainly not his ageing invalid wife, and Babette bent her head low over her drink to hide a smile as they passed by.

Louis was deeply engrossed in a card game when she found him, a large pile of chips on the table before him.

"You see," his eyes lit up with unusual enthusiasm, "my luck has changed."

"It is growing late, Louis. You promised."

He frowned, staring intently at his cards. Did she expect him to leave and break his lucky streak?

"Patience – later."

Babette's lips tightened, conscious of the smile on the face of the man nearest her brother.

"I shall go alone," she dared.

"Enjoy yourself."

She fought down the angry retort which rose to her lips. She wanted to knock the wretched cards from his hands and drag him down to the carnival, but a strict upbringing had taught her to curb impetuosity and a very unladylike temper. The last outburst, she remembered, had earned her a sound spanking, administered by Louis' strong hand on an extremely tender place.

Her head held high, she swept out of the room, collected her cloak and walked quickly down the drive, inwardly seething. A cool breeze blew in from the bayou, too pleasant to ignore, and she cut through the trees to the water's edge, took off her shoes and wandered barefoot over the sand.

Louis was impossible, she decided, but he was not going to spoil her evening.

With a soft laugh she dropped on to the warm sand, staring out across the bayou bathed in moonlight. It had never looked so peaceful before. This was her favourite spot – she would miss it when she married and the chains of family would be replaced by those of a jealously possessive husband. But at least for four whole days while her father and Ralph were away on business, she was free.

"How lovely," she whispered to the tall trees swaying gently above her head.

"I agree," a voice remarked almost in her ear. Spinning round, she discovered that she was not alone. In the bright moonlight she saw a man lounging against one of the many fishing boats lining the beach for miles. A cheroot dangled from his lips.

She fought down the sudden rush of panic, forcing herself to remain seated. She had never been alone with a total stranger before, but he was not to know that, and her mask hid her identity. Apparently he had not come from the town for he wore ordinary clothes, well-cut and expensive – a dazzling white silk cravat was at his throat. He looked every inch a gentleman. Removing the cheroot from his mouth he moved a pace or two towards her, saying:

"Did I startle you? My apologies. I thought you were remarking on the beauty of the scenery." His voice was deep, attractive. She moved back into the shadows conscious of heightening colour.

"I was thinking aloud," she confessed.

"I see." He chuckled and motioned to Sans Souci with a sweep of his arm. "Have you had enough excitement for tonight?"

"How did you know I was there?"

"I saw you – that red dress is very becoming. Are you taking part in the celebrations?"

Babette thought of Louis and his card game and a deep sigh escaped her.

"My brother was to be my escort, but he prefers to gamble and so I came here. I often come here, but during the day – never at night before. I suppose now Sans Souci has been bought I shall no longer be able to ride in the grounds. I am sure the new owner would not like to see me gallop past his windows at six in the morning."

The stranger chuckled again and tossed the cheroot towards the water.

"At such an early hour I think I might find it refreshing."

Babette's head jerked up – staring at him with widening eyes.

"You – you own Sans Souci?"

"Please – don't sound so alarmed – I am perfectly harmless."

"But a gambler –" she protested. She had heard many tales of riverboat gamblers from Louis and the local gossip-mongers. Men of low repute, unscrupulously cheating passengers out of money, jewels, anything they could lay their hands on – and they kept company with women of loose morals with painted faces whose dresses were vulgar and cut far lower than decency allowed. Horrified, she looked down at her own dress and wished she was safely at home.

"Are we so terrible?" he asked in amused tones. Regardless of his clothes, he sat beside her – peering into her face, which she averted instantly. "Oh, now I understand."

"What do you understand?" she asked in a small voice.

"A gambler is not the kind of man you usually associate with – I mean a girl of good family background such as yourself."

Babette was speechless. Her face was covered – how did he know? He could not have recognised her.

"Do you think a mask can hide what you are?" he asked. "Your voice gives you away – the colour in your cheeks. No, I can't see it, but I know it's there. You are afraid to be alone with me. Perhaps such a situation has never occurred before – somehow I think it has not – therefore I will force my company on you no longer." He rose, dusted down his suit and was walking away before Babette fully realised what he had said.

"Monsieur." She jumped to her feet and stood clutching her shoes in one hand, the other stretched out towards him. He stopped and turned and looked at her silently. Slowly she crossed the space between them, aware of the boldness of his gaze – yet not minding it. "You are right – such a situation has never occurred before. It is my only excuse for being so rude. I beg you to overlook it."

"How can I not forgive such an attractive gypsy girl – even if her beauty is half hidden behind a mask."

Babette's fingers strayed to the black velvet. It was a temptation to tear it off and allow him to see her clearly. Sensing her indecision he reached out and drew her hand away.

"No – stay a mystery and intrigue me."

Babette found she was trembling as she slipped on her shoes.

"I must go," she said, but made no move to do so.

The stranger glanced at Sans Souci – then towards the town. In the quietness of the bayou they could clearly hear the sounds of revelry. Babette's heart ached to think how near, yet how far away it was for her.

"A pity to miss it," he murmured. "Of course it'd not be correct to be seen in my company – but you are masked and Mardi Gras is a time to enjoy yourself. Do you not agree?"

Dare she? This had been part of her dream. Why did she hesitate? Louis was fully occupied – no one would take any notice of a gypsy girl with a stranger – probably many people would not know him – Sans Souci had only been open a few weeks.

"You are most kind, Monsieur," she answered. "I accept your invitation – but with one condition."

"Which is?"

"You make no attempt to find out who I am – no one must know. If my father should discover I have been out alone – talked with you –" she broke off, not wishing to contemplate the consequences.

"What colour are your eyes?" he asked.

"Blue – why?"

"I must call you something – it shall be Blue-eyes. As for me, there is no reason why you should not know my name. Grant Tyler – gambler, at your service. Are you still afraid?"

Babette slipped her arm through his, spurred to recklessness by the mockery in his voice.

"I am not a child, Monsieur Tyler," she retorted boldly, but the infuriating smile on his face told her that he thought otherwise.

"Come back to the house. I will order the barouche," Grant said, but she shook her head and gave a soft laugh.

"No, it is too beautiful a night to ride in a carriage. I will take you into town by the back paths. What time is it?"

Grant looked at the gold watch on his waistcoat chain.

"Almost ten."

"Then the processions will have reached the Old Quarter by now . . . you will find that a very exciting part of New Orleans . . ."

"With you, tea on the vicarage lawn would be exciting," Grant returned softly and she quickly stepped back, avoiding the hand outstretched towards her.

"Come along, we don't want to miss it."

She led him into the town by the routes Louis had shown her when they used to ride together in the days before his drinking and gambling occupied all his free time. She had never forgotten them and used them herself frequently, hoping to avoid unnecessary comments being made to her father on how his daughter rode alone – unchaperoned! – in the countryside.

The sound of the river grew louder as she walked quickly, confidently towards Canal Street, which ran at right angles to the bank and cut the city completely in two. Across the other side was the old French Quarter – to her, the prettiest part of New Orleans. The houses here were very old – many were spacious mansions inhabited by aristocratic families who had first come here when New Orleans was the administrative centre of French Louisiana in the 1700s, before it was ceded to Spain. After its return to France in 1800, the bloody terror of the revolution which ravaged Paris and the rest of the country had brought many more to make new lives for themselves in this thriving cotton port.

"New Orleans people certainly know how to enjoy themselves," Grant chuckled as he slipped an arm around her waist to prevent her being swept along in the opposite direction by a crowd of revellers in horned masks. "Where are they off to?"

Babette stared after the figures. She had recognised the Serpent god, Damballa, in his top hat and white gloves and knew there was to be another celebration that evening – in some wooded spot, far from curious eyes. There would be dancing and feasting in the presence of Mamaloi and then they would take a poor defenceless chicken and . . . Grant looked at her curiously.

"I asked who they were, Blue-eyes?"

"Voodoo worshippers. Damballa, the Serpent god and Mamaloi, the High Priestess – the others were followers. It is best we go on . . . we will not be welcome here."

"Well, you did say this was an exciting place." Grant's mocking tone told her he was not a believer, but then he was not a Creole . . . he had never heard the drums in the dead of night or heard Jemima's tales . . .

A riverboat was just pulling away from the harbour when they arrived. She saw her companion's expression grow thoughtful as he paused to light a cheroot. They could clearly hear the sound of laughter from the decks. She suspected he was wishing himself on board.

"She looks like my old boat," he remarked. Why did men always call boats "she", Babette wondered? "I sold her to buy Sans Souci."

"And you are regretting it, perhaps?"

He looked down at her with a smile and a shake of his head.

"I've learned to enjoy the comforts money brings. For the first week, I thought I was the biggest fool God had ever put on this earth to let her go, but now? No, I have no regrets."

They wandered slowly back into the crowded side streets.
Grant bought her some little *estomacs du mulatre*, delicious
ginger cookies and some rice cakes for himself from one of
the many stalls lining the banquette and they laughed at the
sometimes grotesque masks which passed by. Above their
heads the ironwork balustrades were lined with people who
often showered the passers-by with flowers from the balconies they stood on. Grant bent to retrieve one from the
ground and handed it to her with a flourish. She tried to keep
it in her hair, but it would not stay. With sudden daring she
pushed the creamy white magnolia bloom into the neckline of
her dress.

They passed courtyards filled with happy, laughing, singing individuals who invited them in to share their hospitality.
Babette had never felt so happy – so free . . . she lost track of
time. If only the night could go on for ever . . . if only . . .

A buxom Negress thrust two cups of herb tea into their
hands as they stood for a moment listening to the sound of
someone singing on the other side of a stucco wall. Babette
recognised the tune as that of an old Creole love song. How
appropriate for such a night – a night of dreams – a night
when nothing was real. What did it matter . . . ?

They were about to move on when she caught sight of a tall
woman in a bright red blouse and skirt, a spotted red and
white tignon tied around her jet black hair. Her complexion
was flawless and far lighter than those of the women at her
side. Madame Seraphin! Jemima's fortune-teller!

Babette knew her maid doted on every word this woman
said, but had never actually met her. Some of her friends had
been for a consultation and been frightened out of their wits
when the predictions had come true and they had been forced
to swallow their scoffing words. She remembered Mary-
Louise, the daughter of a close neighbour, had been told she
would have two children, both would be born dead – and her
not even married! Two months later she had run off with a
young man from Baton Rouge who had left her when she

became pregnant. Mary-Louise's two boys had been still-born, and she herself had died the following day. Babette had often wondered if Madame Seraphin had omitted that final, terrible prophecy deliberately in order to spare her further pain. There had been others . . . and each one had made her more curious.

Of course she did not believe in fortune-tellers . . . at least she told herself that, but in that instant, as she gazed across the street at the Creole woman seated in her doorway, Babette was seized with an urge to know what life held for her. Had she not met Grant Tyler would she still have wanted to know, she wondered, hesitating.

"And what do you find so fascinating?" Grant asked, following her gaze.

"Not what – who," Babette said, in a low tone, as if Madame Seraphin possessed extra sensitive hearing and might be aware of what she was saying. It was strange that the woman should look across at that very moment to the spot where she stood. "That is Madame Seraphin – she can pre-dict the future."

"The dangerous pastime of rogues and charlatans," Grant returned. "Don't waste your time. Surely you already know what the future holds for a girl of your background? A marriage to the man of your father's choice – the raising of a large family to inherit his business when he has gone . . ."

"Don't," Babette whispered. Did he not know how his words upset her? She did not want these things. Marriage to Ralph – his children. She hated his touch . . . how could she bear to be his wife – his property?

"The prospects do not appeal to you? I'm glad. It would be a pity to waste you on some indolent young southern gentle-man who didn't appreciate what he had in his possession."

"Don't talk like that! You don't have to come with me if you don't believe . . ."

Grant caught her by the arm as she started defiantly across the road.

"Gently, Blue-eyes, do you think I will let you go in there

alone?" As they approached the doorway, the Creole woman stood up and ducked back out of sight behind the patterned curtains.

Babette slowed her pace for a moment only before following, with Grant close on her heels and still holding tightly to her hand. How reassuring his grasp was . . .

The room was lighted only by candles secured in wall holders. The flickering light cast shadows all around them – on the roughly-made altar at the far end where the stone figure of Damballa sat, on the impassive face of the woman beside him, her dark eyes centred on Babette.

"Mademoiselle wishes to know her future?" she asked in soft Creole French. "Whether she will marry the handsome one at her side, perhaps?" Her gaze rested amusedly on the hand which lay passively in Grant's clasp.

"Yes – yes, I want to know the future." Babette hoped she did not sound as nervous as she felt.

Madame Seraphin nodded and held out a hand. She had very long, slender fingers with pointed nails, painted as brilliant a red as the blouse she wore.

"Give me something to hold – something which has been close to you all evening."

Babette wore no jewellery except her golden earrings. She was about to remove them when a scarlet talon was pointed at the flower nestling in the hollow between her breasts.

"Give me that."

With trembling fingers she handed over the magnolia blossom.

"It still retains the warmth of your body," Madame Seraphin said, her features breaking into a satisfied smile. "It tells me much."

Grant gave a heavy sigh but the interruption was ignored. "It is a body which will bring great pleasure to the one who loves you – if he is man enough to possess you."

"M-man," Babette echoed. Was there to be no name?

She stole a sidelong glance at Grant. His narrowed eyes held a mixture of disbelief and amusement. He would not believe one word the woman told her. Was he the one fate had decreed was to be the man who would possess her? It was an exciting thought, but totally impracticable.

Madame Seraphin began to pluck the petals from the flower. Slowly, one by one they fell through her fingers on to the floor. Babette was alarmed to see her begin to frown.

"The omens are not good – too much will happen in a very short space of time. You will be unhappy. Give me your hands."

Wordlessly Babette stretched them out before her. She caught her breath as the Creole woman slowly ran her fingers over the unmarked palms, the soft, perfumed backs and along the well manicured nails. Her touch was ice-cold!

"Soft – too soft," she muttered. "Like you, my little one. He will hurt you . . ."

"The girl is waiting for a prediction on her future," Grant broke in rudely, "or are you waiting to be paid first?"

"Grant – don't," Babette protested, afraid some terrible spell might be cast on him for such impudence. Madame Seraphin did not even look at him.

"There is one who hungers after you, child – who will lay claim to you and teach you the ways of love – the pleasures and also – the heartaches. A pity – a great pity."

"What is?" Babette asked.

"It is a great pity he is not the one you are soon to marry."

"I've heard enough." Grant tossed a silver coin down on to the table beside him, indicating that his patience was at an end.

There was a strange smile on the woman's face as she turned her attention on him for the first time since he had entered.

"I will tell your future free of charge, my violent friend. Life has not been kind to you and she still has some unpleasant times ahead, until the time that you find your salvation in one of great innocence. You may smile – but that time is not far distant. You cannot fight innocence – nor destroy it, however hard you try."

She began to laugh . . . softly at first, but at the distressed look on Babette's face it grew louder, more mocking. "You wanted to know what the fates had in store for you, my grand lady – well, now you know. After tomorrow, neither of you will have any control – any control at all over your own lives. Seraphin has spoken – now go – enjoy yourselves while there is still time."

With a muttered oath, Grant seized Babette by the hand and practically dragged her out into the street again. She found herself trembling as she ran to keep up with his fierce stride. Not until they were on the other side of Canal Street did he slow his pace and allow her to regain her breath.

Madame Seraphin had called him a violent man, Babette thought, watching his chiselled profile in the glare of a match as he lighted a cheroot. How could she have known that – or that she, Babette, was no gypsy girl unless she had the power of second sight. Grant looked at her as she shivered.

"Don't let that witch upset you. She's a fraud – they all are. I've laid my life on the line with the turn of a card and I'm not likely to be frightened by her ramblings. Were you?"

"Of – of course not." She would be hurt, Seraphin had said. By this man? No – that was not possible for their relationship would end with the Mardi Gras. They would never be with each other like this again . . .

"Will you be a gentleman and escort me part of the way back, Monsieur Tyler?" she asked, forcing a smile to her lips. They were almost alone on the street and despite her assurances to the contrary, Seraphin's predictions had alarmed her. She wanted to get back home as quickly as possible.

"But of course, mademoiselle." Grant's flippant tone matched hers. If he sensed her misgivings he did not show it, and her heart warmed towards him. She would never forget him or these wonderful hours in his company. Whatever anyone said about him in the future, she knew he was kind and gentle and a perfect gentleman . . .

CHAPTER
TWO

BABETTE awoke to a brilliantly sunny morning and the realisation she was being persistently shaken.

"Miss B'bette. Breakfast."

"In a while – I'm so tired." She rolled over, blinking
fiercely as the strong white light dazzled her. She felt like a
rag doll. "What time is it, Jemima?"

"Almost noon."

Noon! Babette sat up, staring disbelievingly into her
maid's coal-black features. So late – but then it had been four
in the morning before she returned to the house. Eight hours
since Grant Tyler had held her in his strong arms and they
had danced until she was almost exhausted. Once in the town
where the lights were plentiful, she had found he was disturbingly good-looking. Sunburnt skin and hair thick and black.
A lean mouth that never stopped smiling all evening and
those dark, piercing eyes. Even now she grew hot to think of
their scrutiny. For the first time in her young life she had felt
a woman, even if he did not regard her as such.

She had left him at the beginning of the long St. George
Avenue in the select part of town near her home, and hurried
through the deserted streets, clutching her cloak tightly
around the red dress. The back door of the servants' quarters
was always open – a fact shared only by the servants, Louis
and herself. With her brother's increased drinking habits and
unstable hours it had become necessary for him to be able to
return home unseen and unheard. Another secret kept from
their father.

"I must say you appear remarkably cheerful this morning," Louis commented when she entered the drawing room.

"Afternoon," she corrected smilingly. She was quick to notice the dark circles beneath his eyes – the decanter of whisky and a full glass on the table beside him.

"No lectures, *ma petite*," he said before she could reprove him. "I am in dire need of a stimulant."

"Oh – you lost. Badly?"

"More than I could afford which means I must attempt to win some of it back this evening."

Babette shook her head. If she had stayed, could she have persuaded him to leave earlier?

"Louis, whatever shall I do with you? But I cannot be angry with you today. I am too happy."

"And what man has brought about this miraculous change?" Louis asked with a surprised smile.

"Why must it be a man?"

He laughed, swallowed the whisky in one gulp and replenished the glass to the brim.

"This morning – correction, afternoon – you are looking quite radiant. Only a man could put such a glow into those cheeks. So you did go off on your own, after all. I'm afraid I was rather engrossed in the cards when you turned up. What's his name?"

"I shall not tell you," Babette perched herself on the arm of his chair, moving the decanter out of reach, "Unless you promise me not to take another drink before lunch."

Louis frowned angrily, saw the determination which crept into her eyes and slowly nodded.

"I shall make up for it afterwards," he growled. "Now – who is this wonder man?"

"What if I told you it was Grant Tyler?" She offered the name hesitantly.

"I should warn you not to play with fire. One in the family with burnt fingers is enough."

"Louis," Babette chided gently, "don't talk that way." It was not often he referred to his own past unhappiness and it made her uncomfortable. She hated to think anyone could ever have hurt him. "It is Grant Tyler," she continued. "Have you met him?"

Louis lips twisted into a bitter smile.

"Our paths have crossed. He accepted several of my I.O.U.s last night without a murmur. Is that really who you were with?"

"Until four o'clock this morning."

Babette jumped to her feet – flushed with excitement.

"I've never met anyone like him before. He is most intelligent – for a gambler, I mean. Why did you say I was playing with fire?"

Louis looked up at her thoughtfully. Attired in a full-sleeved silk gown, the long hair coiled elegantly on to the crown of her head, she appeared every inch a lady. Not like last night when she had been wild – provocative, with the light of devilry dancing in her eyes. The kind of woman who would appeal to a man like Grant Tyler.

"I hear he is a man of violent moods," he answered sombrely. "Only a week ago he had an argument with one of the customers at Sans Souci – beat him half to death in a fight and then threw him bodily into the bayou."

Babette paled but stood her ground.

"I thought him quite gentle," she said a trifle stiffly. She had certainly not expected opposition from this quarter.

"Of course he tried to make love to you."

"He did not – Louis, you are insufferable – or are you drunk? I met Monsieur Tyler down by the bayou where I went after you refused to keep your promise to me. We talked for a while – then he offered to escort me to the Mardi Gras and I accepted. He behaved like a perfect gentleman the whole time we were together – he did not even press me for my name. I have promised to meet him again tonight. Are you going to object?"

"I am your brother – not your keeper," he answered. "But be careful, *ma petite*. Now it is a mild flirtation – you find each other amusing – intriguing perhaps, but don't let it go beyond that. If you should be hurt – " he broke off, his face lined with pain. Babette sat beside him, drawing his head against her breast. That was what Madame Seraphin had said.

"Hush, *mon frère*," she murmured, stroking his hair. "It will go no further." But even as she uttered the words she wondered if she was lying.

Grant Tyler was waiting for her that night in the same spot along the beach, sitting on one of the upturned boats. Babette had been running, afraid that he would not be there, but the moment she saw him she stopped and composed herself before walking to his side.

"I thought you might not come," he said rising.

"I promised –"

"Women are well known for their lack of regard to such things," he returned quickly.

"I do not usually break my word, Monsieur Tyler." Babette's voice was indignant. "Perhaps you would rather I had not come?"

"I think you know that is unfair – and untrue." His obvious sincerity overwhelmed her indignation.

"Must we quarrel?" she asked softly.

They began to wander slowly over the sand. Tonight there was no wind and the bayou was quiet – otherwise deserted.

Babette, who had been brooding on Seraphin's and then Louis' observations of her companion, asked unexpectedly,

"Are you a violent man, Monsieur Tyler?"

Grant produced a cheroot from an inside pocket of his jacket, paused to light it and over the flickering flame of the match his eyes met hers, full of unspoken mockery.

"What do you think?"

"I do not know you," she protested, quickly looking away, "it is my brother's opinion, not mine. If you want me to give an opinion – then you must first tell me about yourself."

"Is that fair?" he demanded. "I am not allowed to know your name or see your face. You present yourself to me as a gypsy girl who will vanish out of my life the moment Mardi Gras is over – yet I am expected to furnish you with details of my lurid past." He laughed aloud at her worried expression.

"Lurid was a bad word to use. I see your imagination is already at work. Very well – I will comply with your wishes."

They walked, without noticing time or distance, while he talked of his life before coming to New Orleans. Babette found him to be an excellent conversationalist, describing his travels so vividly to her, that she felt she might actually have been there with him. She had never been further than Baton Rouge in all her twenty years and listened intently to this man who knew so much about the outside world. Among other things she learnt he came originally from Virginia, of a backwoods family, but had spent the last six years as a gambler on the river boats. With such a background she was now sure he was a man of violence and grew surprised to find it did not worry her. She liked his company – the quiet unassuming charm that made her feel at ease with him. If only the Mardi Gras could go on for ever, but then she would also have to go on pretending and she would hate that.

The beach ended abruptly in a long curve sweeping upwards to a steep bank where beyond, silhouetted in the moonlight, were the remains of a derelict mansion.

For years this had been her secret place – her sanctuary – her escape from the respectability the name of St. Clair had forced her to endure. She was twenty years old. She had been told she was beautiful – and intelligent! Why then did her father impose such unbearable restrictions on her life? Did he not think her capable of choosing her own friends with due regard for his position? She had been schooled to be the mistress of the house since her beloved mother had died when she was only ten years old – yet now that she considered herself able to take charge with pride and dignity, she was deliberately sheltered from friends and relatives alike – any-one who might have the slightest influence on her thinking.

Everyone – except Ralph Weldon. Since he had become her father's business partner, his attitude towards her had changed considerably. There were times nowadays when he treated her as if she was his property. She knew that was how he thought of her – a possession – another item to be acquired with the same lack of feeling as when he purchased another piece of porcelain or jade.

The old plantation house which adjoined Sans Souci offered a welcome retreat from the world. She would ride there alone and spend hours wandering through the deserted rooms, trying to imagine what it must have been like in its glory. Part of the roof had gone and many of the windows had been broken by mischievous children, but the rooms still held a magic all their own and their magnetism never failed to draw her back.

She would stand on the dusty mahogany floor in the once magnificent ballroom and close her eyes and hear the sound of lilting music, see the crinolined ladies gliding past her in the arms of handsome Southern gentlemen. How she envied them their freedom! The only escorts she had ever known were Ralph and Louis.

The heady perfume of magnolia blossom invaded the rooms through cracked or broken window panes. The cascading wisteria which crept over the balconies and long galleries had, in places, taken over so completely that very little of the wrought ironwork could be seen. The gardens were overgrown with weeds, only the tall oaks which lined the driveway and the terraced path down to the edge of the river, seemed to have retained any of the dignity pertaining to the old house.

They were like silent, watchful sentinels, protecting what remained of the once grand plantation which had survived fire, flood and even a slave insurrection, so Babette had heard, only to fall victim to the overwhelming burden of taxes levied on the unfortunate occupants.

How she hoped that one day someone would love this place as she did – buy it – bring it back to life. One day perhaps another girl would stand on the balcony in the grand bedroom and listen to the shrill whistle of the paddle-steamers en route to Baton Rouge, watch the smoke from their chimney stacks climbing high into the blue sky.

The view from that window was the best in the house.

Babette always went there when she was feeling particularly low. The river was always busy – steamers, fishing boats, huge-sailed vessels departing with cotton for England. She would watch them and dream of another time when she would leave New Orleans and visit some of the exciting places she had only read about in books. Surely she could not stay in this one place all her life? There had to be something more than to marry and raise a family . . . or was she so different from other girls of her age?

Across the river, new palatial houses had been built on the high ground now protected from flood by the recently erected levees. Babette had been allowed to call on the new neighbours, duly chaperoned by Louis. She had walked on the green lawns amid beautiful strutting peacocks and found herself comparing them to the delicate, sheltered womenfolk who lived in these wealthy mansions. Louis had laughed when she told him of her comparison, but he knew she had not been joking. He sensed her frustration, but could do nothing to alleviate it. Only the old plantation house could do that . . . and now that, too, was another thing forbidden to her. It belonged to Grant Tyler . . .

"Goodness – we have walked at least a mile," Babette declared. "That's the old plantation house belonging to Sans Souci. Have you seen it?"

"Unfortunately I have not had the time. Is it completely ruined?"

"Practically. The previous owners moved out some eight or nine years ago. Sans Souci was built to take its place. It was a beautiful house. The plantations were extremely rewarding, but they are badly in need of care and attention." She turned on him excitedly. "Come and see it – perhaps you will want to rebuild it and become a rich plantation owner instead of a gambler."

"I'm a Virginian backwoodsman, not a southern gentleman," Grant retorted dryly, but he followed her to where the steep banking commenced. For some reason her suggestion aroused a strange excitement in him.

"Can you manage?"

He reached out, intending to hold her firmly round the waist while she gained a foothold, but at the first contact of his hand against her body she recoiled away from him with a startled gasp.

"Gently, Blue-eyes, I only meant to help you. Why are you so afraid? Have I not conducted myself as a gentleman at all times?" A soft chuckle rose from deep in his throat. "So that's it – you thought I was about to kiss you."

Babette moved away from him until her back was against the bank and she could go no further.

"I thought no such thing," she returned falteringly.

"You are the prettiest liar I've ever met, Blue-eyes," Grant said in soft Creole French. She was too surprised to reply and could only stand trembling before him – ashamed at her lack of trust – afraid of the stranger suddenly confronting her. She had forgotten how familiar he was with the old tongue.

"It's obvious you regard me as one kind of *bête noire*, I should hate you to be disappointed," he said with sardonic humour and swept her hard against him, holding her in a firm embrace from which escape was impossible. She discovered all attempts to free herself were useless. His lips closed over hers – and met with stubborn resistance. Raising his head, he looked down at her masked face. "It would be so easy to find out who you are now," he warned.

"Oh – no – you promised," she whispered, aghast that her identity might be revealed.

"That was yesterday. Tonight you must pay my price – one kiss, given willingly."

Babette's heart failed her. He did not realise what he was asking of her.

"I cannot – please, let me go."

Grant shook his head, adamant in his decision.

"My price or the mask comes off," he threatened.

He knew she would have to agree and waited patiently for the tenseness to go out of her body. It was soft and warm beneath his touch and he was in no hurry to release her.

"Very well." Her answer was barely audible. Eyes tightly closed she raised her face to his and for a long moment was forced to endure her first real kiss.

"I can remember more enthusiastic responses," Grant mocked, drawing away, and was alarmed to see her slide on to the sand at his feet, her face buried in her hands.

"I hate you," she sobbed. "Go away – please, go away!"

"Leave you alone – out here?"

"It will be far safer than to stay with you," she retorted tearfully.

Grant knelt beside her and slipped a comforting arm around her shoulders. Immediately she grew tense.

"Blue-eyes, believe me, I mean you no harm. I had no idea you would be so upset." He tilted up her chin and swore under his breath at the sight of the tears brimming in her eyes. "Have you never been kissed before?"

"Never like that," Babette whispered.

"Was it so terrible?" He was no longer laughing at her, but was genuinely concerned at the distress his action had brought about. She became very still and quiet, staring at him. Her answer came after a long while.

"No – it makes me afraid. Louis, my brother, said this was nothing more than a flirtation, but when you kissed me I felt" – she coloured hotly – "something I have never known before." She ran a hand across her eyes, dashing away the last traces of tears. "I am ashamed of being so foolish. You are right to regard me as a child."

"I think of you as a child?" Grant said in startled tones. "Indeed I do not. You are all woman, Blue-eyes."

Babette caught her breath at the look in his eyes. Ralph had never looked at her this way, held her tightly against him and kissed her so ardently. To him she was another pretty ornament to be added to his collection – put on a shelf and admired from a distance.

Grant's arms slid round her back and he bent towards her, his mouth once more seeking hers.

"No – no –"

He closed his ears to her protests and this time there was no resistance. Her lips flared to life with an eagerness to match his own and all thought of Ralph vanished from her mind. He kissed her forehead, cheeks, throat, mouth – again and again – whispering the soft endearments she had always dreamed her man would whisper. She felt as if the ground swayed beneath her feet.

"Please, Monsieur Tyler. Grant – you must let me go."

Reluctantly Grant obeyed, his expression serious as he watched her smooth back her dishevelled hair. She was such a child in years, yet he found her innocence pleased him, and made him regret the past affairs that had meant nothing to him.

"This cannot end tomorrow, Blue-eyes. We must meet again. I must know your name."

"No."

Babette scrambled to her feet, evading his outstretched hand. "Louis was right, it is only a flirtation. When we part we will soon forget each other. Our lives can never be one."

Grant rose to stand beside her, frowning heavily.

"Do you really believe that?"

"I must – because," she faltered over the words, but they had to be spoken, "I am not free."

His glance swept down to her ringless hand, his mouth tightening.

"You are not married?"

"No. Engaged. My fiancé is away."

"And so you decided to amuse yourself with the first man who came along," Grant snapped bitterly. "A mild flirtation – to last exactly three days. I've a good mind –" his hand stretched out menacingly towards her mask.

"Tear it off," Babette cried defiantly, "if you know so little of women not to believe I had no intention of flirting with you or anyone. I wanted to dance in the streets, and enjoy myself like any other girl. You are a gambler, you must realise how I feel – know what I have risked. Take it off if that is what you want. Prove to me the kind of man you really are."

Grant's hand fell away.

"If I did you would hate me. I cannot risk that happening. You have spirit, Blue-eyes, remind me not to provoke you again. Next time I may have my eyes clawed out." He swung around towards the bank. "I would still like to take a look at my property. Will you come with me?"

Babette hesitated, then placed her hand in his and together they scrambled up the slope and across the uneven plantation land to the empty shell of the house.

"You say Sans Souci was built to take the place of this house?" Grant stared up at the overgrown galleries, a half-smile touching his lips. If his friends could see him now, he mused. The owner of not one, but two houses and a plantation to equal any of the well-to-do families in New Orleans.

"Soon after Sans Souci was completed, poor Monsieur Renaud went bankrupt. It was rumoured he could not afford the second house, but had had it built for his new wife who was very much younger than he was. When he lost all his money she left him. He shot himself after receiving an enormous tax demand which he could not meet. Poor man . . . to lose all this."

Babette gave a sigh as she looked around her. Down by the edge of the water, the Spanish moss fell from the trees like a graceful curtain, protecting them from prying eyes – or so she liked to think. She did not want anyone ever to know what this place meant to her – no one except perhaps the man at her side, whose sudden intrusion into her closed little world had made it impossible for it to be the same again.

"Don't tell me you like it here?" Grant asked, staring down at her amusedly. "Don't tell me why – let me guess. You have illusions of grandeur . . . pretending you are mistress here, entertaining your guests on the terraced lawns, waited on by dozens of lackeys who jump at your every command."

He made it sound awful. That was not the way she imagined it at all, Babette thought indignantly.

"Perhaps if you were to look inside, you might understand

exactly what it is I feel," she suggested. "Even a Virginian backwoodsman must have a little imagination."

He gave a soft laugh and, still holding possessively to her hand, walked on into the house.

A gentle evening breeze from the bayou invaded the interior of the house. Just over the threshold Grant stopped and allowed his eyes to become accustomed to the gloom.

"This way." Without hesitation Babette led him through into the drawing room, to a table where she knew there was an oil lamp.

"Perhaps it will still light." She hoped so. She wanted him to see everything the house had to offer.

She had never been here at night before. As Grant took out his match case and a tiny flame of light sprang to life between his cupped hands, she caught her breath. Long shadows, like strange misshapen figures, sprang out at them from every corner of the room. Voodoo spirits, she thought in panic, suddenly recalling to mind the eerie stories Jemima had often told her about the black art practised by so many of the coloured slaves, but then as Grant lighted the lamp and held it high in front of him, the yellow light chased away her ghosts and she heard herself give a shaky laugh.

"Frightened, Blue-eyes?" the man at her side asked softly.

Not with you, she almost replied and stopped herself luckily before the words were uttered.

"Of course not . . ."

"Then give me a guided tour. I admit, I am fascinated."

Babette needed no more encouragement. She took him from room to room, from the depths of the cellars to the small, barred windowed attic and then down the cobwebbed staircase to the servants' quarters and the enormous kitchen with its black cooking range, covered in inches of dust.

"It's quite a place," Grant drawled. Depositing the lamp, which was beginning to flicker slightly, on the table in front of him, he produced a familiar long cheroot and lighted it. Babette was more than a little disappointed by his lack of enthusiasm.

"You don't like it?" she ventured to ask.

"If I was a family man with more money than I knew what to do with, and an adoring wife dedicated to giving me hordes of children, it would suit me down to the ground . . ."

"You are laughing at me."

"Now why should I do that? What good is it to me? I have Sans Souci and that's cost enough to put back on its feet. Look at this kitchen – don't you think I'd feel rather foolish sitting down here all alone?"

"The master eats in the dining room, not in the kitchen," Babette returned appalled.

"There you are – I don't even know how to act the grand-seigneur. Of course if I had someone to teach me . . ."

He was laughing at her, Babette realised. From what she had so far seen of him he was quite capable of being whatever he chose – gambler – gentleman – country boy . . . Why was he so loath to admit the prospects this house held out for him? She watched his face grow suddenly thoughtful as his eyes came to rest on the stove.

"Now if my mother was still alive . . ." his voice was so quiet he might have been talking to himself instead of to her . . . "how she would have loved to cook at that great iron monster."

"She is dead?" Babette asked, her tone matching his. She did not want to disturb his new train of thought. It was the first time he had ever mentioned any family.

"Life killed her . . . the responsibility of bringing up six children, mostly alone. My father died when I was twelve. That made me the eldest – the breadwinner . . . the man of the house. My two sisters died of the fever before they reached the age of five – one of my brothers went the following year because we were too poor to afford a doctor. What little we had went on food because drought had ruined the crops or our traps had been looted by neighbours. It was dog eat dog in those days . . . and it killed her. Every day I watched her die a little more until she just gave up . . . what a waste!"

"Perhaps to her it was a life well lived," Babette answered. "She sounds as if she had a fine family . . ."

"And what would you know about it in your fine house, with servants at your beck and call? When have you ever gone hungry?" Grant snapped and she stepped back from the anger in his eyes, frightened by the change in him. The moment passed as quickly as it had come however. The anger vanished and he began to smile again as the lamp flickered and threatened to die.

"It's time we were leaving."

Babette led the way back upstairs. He replaced the lamp and followed her to the front door. His hand lingered for a moment on the brass handle as he swung it closed behind him.

"If I was to become a respectable southern gentleman, Blue-eyes, would you visit me here?"

Babette stared at him intently, but his face was in the shadows. There was nothing in his voice to tell her he was still making fun of her suggestion, but she decided she was not going to take the chance of more ridicule.

"Suitably chaperoned, of course, monsieur," she said pertly, dropping a curtsey. "I would be delighted."

Grant did not answer. As they began to walk back alongside the river, Babette found herself wondering if he had, in fact, been serious after all?

"I will not go," Babette declared for the third time as the clock struck seven the following evening.

Louis looked up from his book with a sigh.

"You said he is expecting you."

"He is. I am to have dinner with him at Sans Souci. It's our last meeting, but Louis, it will only make matters worse if I go."

"You are going," her brother said firmly and fetched her cloak himself. "I warned you not to play with fire. You ignored me, and now you must take your medicine. Have dinner with him, say your farewells and shut him out of your life from the moment you part. With luck Ralph will never know of this little episode."

"I don't care if he does," Babette flung back over her shoulder and the front door banged loudly behind her departing figure.

Babette's steps faltered as the house came into view. She halted in the driveway and was turning to go back home when a Negro stepped out of the shadows in front of her. At a glance she saw that his livery was that of Sans Souci.

"Massa Tyler sent me to escort you to the house," he said, and gave her a beaming smile.

"How do you know I am the lady expected?" she asked, and then realised Grant Tyler had probably given him a full description to make sure she kept their last appointment. "Never mind. Lead the way and I will follow."

She was shown into a luxuriously furnished drawing room, where Grant was in the act of pouring himself a drink. He saw her and reached for another glass. His gaze moved past her to the Negro.

"Thank you, Sam, you can go, but make sure we are not disturbed."

Grant advanced towards her, took her cloak and led her across to the table before the fire.

"I told my housekeeper only the best was good enough for you and she assures me this is a banquet fit for a queen. Come, drink your aperitif, then we must completely demolish all this food – if we don't, her feelings will be hurt!"

"I am honoured." The words were inadequate, but Babette could find nothing suitable to say. As if he sensed her troubled frame of mind Grant chatted amiably throughout dinner until gradually she began to relax.

Afterwards they sat on the velvet cushioned couch, enjoying their brandies.

"The house is full again tonight," Grant remarked cheerfully. "I wonder how many will dare return tomorrow without a mask to hide who they really are."

Babette flushed.

"Am I included in that statement?"

"You most of all. Are you in love with this man you are going to marry, Blue-eyes?"

"Does it matter? After tonight we must forget each other. What we feel now is not important."

"Such things come hard to a man like me," Grant's voice hardened slightly. "I'm used to taking what I want."

Babette felt herself grow uncomfortable. One moment he was kind and gentle, the next she was afraid of him, not knowing what to expect. Had Louis been right all along?

"You would not – " she faltered, "you could not –" the words refused to come.

Grant rose to refill their glasses. A peal of laughter from below echoed throughout the quiet of the room.

"Could not – what?" he asked deliberately.

Babette took her drink from him and sipped it as she concentrated fiercely on the intricate design on the stem of the glass. She dared not look at him.

Forcing her voice to be casual she said,

"Louis was most concerned when I told him your name –"

"Because I am a man of violent moods," he interposed, "but you were not going to say that."

"He was afraid you would make love to me," she blurted out.

"The thought had occurred to me," Grant replied with a calmness that took her breath away, and the blood drained from her face with such startling rapidity that he grew alarmed, and hastened to add, "I used the past tense, and I have not made love to you, have I?"

"No."

"Good. Now we have established the fact, perhaps we can return to my previous question. Are you in love with your fiancé?"

"I am fond of him."

"That is not love. Therefore it is a marriage of convenience."

"No, not exactly – we are fond of each other. I was engaged

to him when I was born. It is an old custom among our people."

"One I detest," Grant interrupted fiercely. "I suppose he is older than you?"

"Fourteen years."

"My God! He's more like an elder brother. Is that the kind of marriage you want?"

Babette blinked back unhappy tears. Why was he making it harder for them both?

"I have been brought up to obey my father in all things," she returned. "It is his dearest wish I should marry R – the man he has chosen for me. They are good friends. He knows I will be happy."

"Will you?" Grant glared at her, and her discomfort grew. She wanted to run out of the room, away from this man who seemed determined to wreck her marriage – her life – yet she stayed. She had to because everything he said was the truth. He was voicing her own nagging doubts and suspicions. Could she ever find happiness with Ralph when Grant Tyler had so forcefully pushed his way into her life? Before, there had been a chance – now it was impossible. The realisation brought her little comfort. Whatever he said, however hard he convinced her, she still was not free. Her father would never agree to a liaison with a gambler, not after the unfortunate affair involving Louis.

Despondently she looked up into Grant's angry face.

"My future has been planned, we must not try to change it. You do not know the unhappiness it could bring to many people. We agreed to see each other for the days of Mardi Gras – they are over." She rose and drew on her cloak. Grant made no attempt to stop her, but his eyes pleaded with her to stay. "I bid you goodbye – Monsieur Tyler. I will never forget you. You have made me so happy."

"Do you really believe it can end – here and now?" Grant's expression was calm – masking the tumult raging inside him. If he took her in his arms and begged her to remain – No, that might drive her away for ever. She was not like the other women he had known. For the present he had to let her go. "Look in your heart, Blue-eyes, and remember the way I kissed you. It isn't over and I won't say goodbye, *mais au revoir, seulement*."

Babette began to run the moment she was out of the house. Along the driveway and into the crowded streets, pushing through the merrymakers, heedless of their curious glances. She continued running even when a violent stabbing pain pierced her side and she could scarcely breathe – not stopping until the sanctuary of her room where she collapsed across the bed and gave way to a flood of tears.

"*Ma petite*, in heaven's name, what has happened?"

Louis came into the room an hour later to find her crying as if her heart would break.

"Go away."

"I will do nothing of the kind. Sit up and tell me what has caused you to weep so."

Slowly Babette drew herself up on one elbow. Lighting the lamp he sat down beside her, staring with astonishment into her distraught features.

"I love him," she burst out and waited for the storm of retribution she felt sure must come. However, Louis was silent, prompting her to add, "Do you not understand what I am saying? I am soon to marry Ralph, but I am in love with Grant Tyler."

"Are you sure?"

Her eyes glowed for a moment remembering the touch of his lips on hers, abruptly clouding with the realisation she would never again experience such ecstasy.

"As sure as a woman can be over such matters."

"Then you are to meet him again?"

Sadly Babette shook her head. "No, Louis. It is over."

"As easily as snapping your fingers," Louis retorted.

"You sound like Monsieur Tyler. After dinner he lectured me, accusing me of flirting with him because I was bored during Ralph's absence. He said it could not end so abruptly between us."

"If you love him it can't."

Babette clutched at her brother's hand. Why would he not give her the advice she needed? Was he afraid she might follow in his footsteps?

"These past days have been the happiest of my life and the memory of them is pleasant. He knows nothing of my feelings, but if I saw him again I doubt if I could keep them from him and my marriage to Ralph would never take place. No, it has been a clean break, Louis, it is for the best. Besides," she made a feeble attempt to laugh, "would you like Grant Tyler as a brother-in-law? His reputation alone would ruin our family."

"Would you care if you were together?"

"Really, Louis, I do believe you are on his side."

"Anyone's side, except Ralph's," Louis returned, and wandered across to the window to stare out at the deserted avenue lined with trees. If someone did not intervene Babette's life would certainly be ruined.

"Oh, well, if you are determined! You are a fool, *ma petite*," he said, and went to bed.

CHAPTER
THREE

BABETTE received no response to her urgent knocking on
Louis' door next morning at half-past six. When she went in
and tried to rouse him, he had forgotten his promise to ride
with her. He only grunted, buried his head in the pillows and
promptly fell asleep again. She went riding alone – determined to prove to herself that nothing had changed. This was
her usual routine. It had been for years and would probably
continue to be so long after she became Ralph's wife. He
loathed horses – he preferred ships; ships and rare china
figurines. Babette shuddered, but the cause was not the keen
early morning air. She was comparing herself with one of his
cold treasures and shocked to find so little difference between
them.

The tears threatened to flow again. She wheeled her horse
about and allowed it free rein. Its stride did not falter as it
cleared the steep bank and galloped towards the derelict
plantation house. Another horse was tethered outside the
ruins and she reined in, at first thinking that Louis had
changed his mind and taken a short cut to meet her, but on
closer inspection she did not recognise the white stockinged
bay as belonging to their stables. She turned, searching for its
rider, and saw Grant Tyler emerging from inside the house.

"You!" She was too startled to say more.

His gaze swept her from head to toe, taking in the well-cut
riding skirt and expensive silk blouse, so demure after the
low-cut gypsy dress. The black hair braided into one thick
plait fell over her left shoulder and was secured by a large
blue bow. He drew in his breath at the flawless creamy
complexion, hidden until now by the velvet mask.

"You are more beautiful than I imagined, Blue-eyes," he

murmured and the caress in his tone sparked off her temper.

"How dare you follow me! We agreed it was over."

"You agreed," Grant retorted quickly, "and I did not follow you. Are you denying you sent me this?"

Babette's anger dissolved as she stared at the piece of paper he thrust towards her. In Louis' familiar scrawl were the words, *"Bayou St. Michael. 7 a.m."*

"I did not write this."

"Oh – then who did?"

"My brother." Now she understood Louis' reluctance to leave his bed.

Grant regarded her with a puzzled frown.

"I think I am going to like your brother," he said, "but why has he intervened? Is he against your marriage?"

Did Louis want her to break her engagement? she wondered. It had never been mentioned, but then she had never fallen in love before.

"Louis is an optimist," she said ruefully.

Grant reached up to clasp her around the waist and she slid unprotestingly out of the saddle into his arms. He did not attempt to kiss her, but gently laid her cheek against his shoulder, content to hold her and know she did not want to run away. He had never loved any woman so completely before and for the second time he regretted the other women who had been in his life.

"Louis is very wise," he said. "He understands how we feel."

Babette raised her head, searching his face.

"Yes, he understands," she said softly. "Grant, do you want to marry me?"

"Are you thinking I only want to set you up as my mistress in a nice quiet back street and visit you after a hectic evening at Sans Souci?" He was smiling as he spoke, but she grew very pale and the smile vanished. "Damn it – do I have to dot the i's and cross the t's for you! In the past I've had little time for women. I'm not a saint – what man is – but there's never been a girl in my life has come to mean as much to me as you.

If you think it's better we don't meet for a while for fear of gossip, then I'll agree, but I intend to have you for my wife however long you make me wait."

"Oh, Grant!" Colour flooded in a scarlet wave over Babette's face. "I love you!"

"Then nothing will stand in our way."

He kissed her tenderly at first, then more passionately, bruising her mouth with kisses that excited, yet alarmed her. She knew so little of love, she had no idea how her complete surrender inflamed Grant's desire. During the past few days he had guarded his actions for fear of frightening her, but now he gave way to his feelings without restraint – almost ruthlessly, driven by a force he had never experienced before. Yet it was he who drew back and denied himself the pleasure of possessing her.

Babette lay trembling against him, more bewildered than ashamed, at the great new flood of emotions which had taken hold of her. Suddenly the colour ebbed from her cheeks.

"Grant – oh, forgive me, I am shameless."

He drew her against him, kissing her this time without passion.

"No, it was my fault. I am older in knowledge as well as years."

"I know so little," Babette whispered.

"Time enough to learn when we are married," Grant said gently. "Believe me, these few moments have shown me how perfect our life together will be."

"Have you considered what will happen when I break my engagement? Father may still refuse his permission for us to marry."

"Will you defy him?"

"If I must, but it would hurt him terribly. As it is, he may turn me out of the house without a chance to explain. He's afraid of a scandal. It could ruin him. He's Etienne St. Clair."

A low whistle escaped Grant's lips.

"Owner of the biggest shipping line in New Orleans. No

wonder you kept your identity a secret. By the way – must I continue to call you 'Blue-eyes' after we are married?"

"My name is Babette – but I prefer 'Blue-eyes', especially the way you say it. Oh, Grant, hold me. I am afraid this is a dream and you will suddenly vanish."

Grant cradled her in his arms and lay back on the grass. It had been a long time since he had known such peace and this was only the beginning. There would be other days like this and nights filled with the warmth and passion only love can bring.

"Where shall we live, Grant?" Babette asked. She too was thinking of the future.

"Sans Souci."

"But what if father objects to the marriage, he might make it difficult for us."

Grant's lips brushed her forehead.

"If you feel life will be unpleasant here, I can always sell the house, or leave someone to run it. We'll go to St. Louis – Philadelphia – anywhere you want."

"You would do that – for me?" Babette asked.

Grant held her at arms' length, an expression of great tenderness on his face.

"There is nothing I would not do to make you happy," he answered sincerely.

They rode back together along the bayou, hand in hand, Grant seriously contemplating the building of another plantation house for himself and his bride; Babette preparing a defence against her father's wrath.

"When will you tell him?" Grant asked before they parted. "Your fiancé, I mean."

"As soon as he returns tomorrow, father too."

"If there is trouble of any kind, don't hesitate to come to me. If the worst happens, we can always elope on the packet steamer and be married at sea. When will I see you again?"

"Unless anything goes wrong or father wishes to see you – then we must not see each other for at least a week." Grant's face became grim and she leant to kiss away the frown furrowing his forehead. "It must be so, *mon cher*, leave it to me."

"It is a long time," he ventured.

"I know, but at the end of it I hope to come to you with father's blessing."

"A week, then," Grant agreed, "but unless you come to me by then or send word, I shall come looking for you."

His words thrilled Babette. Here was a love beyond her wildest dreams. Taking her leave of him she galloped off, eager to have her brother hear the wonderful news. Grant watched her out of sight before turning his horse on to the path leading up to Sans Souci. Everything was perfect, life seemed suddenly worth living, he thought. Then why did he feel such apprehension at his parting with Babette. It was as if a dark cloud had abruptly obscured the sun.

Louis appeared, framed in the doorway, as Babette cantered into the courtyard, motioning to her to dismount quickly and join him. She ran to him, throwing her arms excitedly around his neck.

"You are the best brother a girl could have," she burst out. "Oh, Louis, I never knew what it was to be alive before and it's all thanks to you."

"Hush." He laid a hand across her mouth. "We are in for a storm, *ma petite*. Our father decided to return home this morning instead of tomorrow, and he had not been at home for more than an hour before Ralph arrived – not in a good humour, I might add. The two of them have been in the study ever since. I tried to hear their conversation through the door, but they are talking too quietly."

"But why?" Babette asked puzzledly. "They have been together these past three days – unless," she broke off, her eyes growing wide in alarm. "Do you think someone recognised me at the Mardi Gras and told Ralph?"

Before Louis could answer, the study door at the far end of the passage opened, and Etienne St. Clair stepped into view.

"I wish to speak with you, Babette – you too, Louis."

Babette's heart sank at the sight of her father's forbidding expression. It was one she knew well, warning her of an unpleasant time ahead. Louis' arm crept around her shoulders as she stumbled forward into the room.

"Sit," Etienne St. Clair ordered, closing the door behind them. They sought the nearest available seating and waited apprehensively.

"I trust you enjoyed your ride, Babette," Ralph Weldon said, turning from the window. He had been standing there so quiet and still, she had not noticed him. Now she turned to acknowledge his presence and she knew something was indeed wrong by the harsh lines around his mouth. With his short, blond hair and fair colouring, he was often mistaken for less than his thirty-four years, but as she looked at him, Babette longed to be with Grant again.

"I did indeed, thank you," she replied politely. "The morning air is most invigorating –"

"Especially after a previous hectic evening," he broke in sarcastically.

Babette gasped and glanced at her brother in dismay. So she had been recognised.

"If you have something to say, I suggest you say it outright," Louis said coldly. "I do not like your insinuations."

"Be quiet." Their father made an attempt to sound stern, but failed. He was a fussy little man, with a small pointed beard and equally small, well-cared-for moustache. The pince-nez perched precariously on his nose, wobbled as he spoke, then fell, to dangle by his side on a long piece of black ribbon. He was a dear, Babette decided, and always had been, but he was forever being dominated, first by Ralph's father, now by Ralph himself. A weak heart was no added incentive to stand on his own two feet. She looked up at her fiancé with a surprisingly demure expression.

"La, Ralph, I do believe you have been listening to gossip. How could you, and about me, too!"

"That is why I listened," came the quick retort. "As it happens, my source of information is extremely reliable. I trust you enjoyed yourself at the Mardi Gras, my dear?"

"And why not? Have I not done so every year since I was a child!" Babette retorted. Inwardly she sighed with relief. At least he did not know of her audacious costume or the man who had partnered her when she danced in the streets.

"But never have you mixed with riff-raff –"

"Since when has my company become distasteful?" Louis ignored his father's angry glare and poured himself a drink. "You see – I escorted Babette every evening. Did I not, *ma petite?*"

Babette chose her words with care.

"Louis is always my escort on such occasions," she answered and neither Ralph nor their father noticed she had not strictly confirmed her brother's statement.

"I see."

Ralph left the window to stand beside her. "And I suppose it was Louis who you were seen kissing so – so ardently beside the bayou early this morning."

"We are close, you know," Louis laughed. White with rage, Ralph appealed to Etienne.

"She is your flesh and blood. I demand you make her admit it. I want to know who this man is."

"That you will not learn from me, at least, not yet," Babette answered, not giving her father a chance to speak. "I admit it, Ralph, I was with a man, the man I am going to marry. Our engagement is at an end. There is nothing you can do to make me change my mind, and if father objects too, even when he knows all the facts, then I shall leave the house."

"And go to your lover?"

Babette laid a detaining hand on Louis' shoulder as he attempted to rise. "No, he wants us to argue, to make the whole thing cheap. He is not my lover, Ralph, he is a gentleman and I love him. Yes, I shall go to him if I have to."

"Babette – my child – what are you saying!" Etienne St. Clair was staring at her aghast. "You cannot love this man. Who is he? What is he to have turned you against Ralph in this manner?"

"I will tell you his name when Ralph has gone," Babette said firmly.

"Perhaps it would be better to leave us alone," Etienne said to Ralph, shrugging his shoulders. "*Mon dieu* – is this house never to be the same again!"

Ralph lowered himself into a nearby chair, smiling complacently.

"I regret I cannot do that." Eyes glinting cruelly, he stared at Babette. "I am afraid, my dear, you will have to forget your lover. I'm not releasing you from our engagement for many reasons which we will not discuss at this moment. You see, I happen to know a great deal about this family – especially the little indiscretions you have all been so careful to conceal. Unless you give me your word here and now to marry me and never see this man again – and make no attempt to contact him before the wedding, I shall be forced to reveal everything I know."

Babette heard Louis mutter a string of oaths and clutched desperately at his arm as he struck out at Ralph's sardonic features. Nothing will stand in our way, Grant had said, his voice full of confidence, but then they had both underestimated Ralph Weldon and the secret he knew which could wreck the happiness of her family.

Numb with shock, she sat motionless, hands clasped tightly in her lap, listening to Ralph and the impossible conditions to which he expected her to agree. No further contact was to be made with her new associate, as he called Grant, and the wedding would now take place within a week. instead of in a month.

A week, she thought, dazedly. By then she was to have been with Grant, planning their future, once more enjoying his kisses. And her father, did he have nothing to say? Could he remain silent while his daughter was being blackmailed into marriage, the very thought of which turned her stomach? Louis sat with his head between his hands and she feared a sudden outburst of violent temper.

"What if I refuse your ultimatum?" she demanded icily.

Ralph's gaze lingered on the proud tilt of her chin, thinking how pleasant it was going to be to bring her down off her pedestal.

"Tonight I shall be the dejected suitor," he mocked. "Probably I might drink too much in a crowded place and inadvertently let slip Louis' grisly secret. Really, my dear, do you think you have a choice in the matter?"

She did not answer and he frowned impatiently. "It seems I must tell you just how desperate I am. I fulfilled my father's deathbed request and went into partnership with your father, to carry on our strong ties of friendship as he put it; a most profitable venture. Regrettably, however, I am now penniless. These last few years I have taken to overspending with the result I'm heavily in debt. Your dowry will help matters a great deal and then, in four or five months' time, I feel I may be able to persuade my generous father-in-law to make me sole owner of the St. Clair shipping line. We have already discussed it –"

"But you agreed to buy me out." Etienne rose from his chair, pale and trembling visibly.

Ralph eyed him contemptuously.

"That was before Babette chose to make trouble for me." His tone softened, and she forced herself to remain calm as he waited expectantly for her reply. "Well, what's it to be?"

"Refuse him," Louis said harshly. "For God's sake, *ma petite*, I am not worth such a sacrifice."

"No, you must not," her father gasped out anxiously. "Think of the disgrace upon our house. The name of St. Clair dragged in the mud, all because my son –"

"Papa!" Babette silenced him with a frosty stare. "I know what I must do, but it's not for you or our name. Yes, Ralph, I will marry you – but I will never be your wife. If you attempt to touch me I will leave you and chance the consequences. You are getting the best of the bargain, even this way. Money, the uniting of two powerful family names, perhaps the full ownership of the Line if father is too weak to refuse it, as I expect he will be."

"You are asking a difficult thing of me, Babette – you were not meant to be alone – unloved. You would not be thinking of seeking solace with your lover, by any chance?"

"No – I have given my word. It will be as you wish."

Ralph nodded slowly. It would not do any harm to comply with her wishes for the moment. Once they were married she would soon learn to submit to his domination.

"Very well, I agree. Now, if you will all excuse me, I think I shall seek out Father Marcel and make the necessary arrangements. A week or so in Baton Rouge may change your mind about me, Babette."

Louis leapt from the couch as Ralph drew level, his hands gripping the other's jacket.

"You heard my sister, Weldon. Now hear me good. If you lay one finger on her I'll kill you."

Ralph shot an amused glance over his shoulder into Babette's horrified face.

"Your brother is becoming most impetuous – but boring. Tell him to release me before I knock him down."

"I think not," Louis answered in a dangerously low voice, and there was an undertone which caused Ralph to look at him closely. The hatred Louis felt for him was mirrored in his eyes; a hatred, Ralph decided, might come from an unstable mind – or one continually warped by liquor. It would not be wise to aggravate it.

"Babette has my promise," he said. "I can find my pleasures elsewhere."

"Ralph! Wait – a word with you." Etienne hurried after him as he strode from the room, leaving Babette and Louis staring at each other in silent anguish.

"For me, wasn't it?" Louis broke the silence first. "You promised for my sake. *Ma chère*, what have you done?"

"Please, Louis," Babette said quietly, "say no more about it. I was a fool to think Grant and I could be together. I only hope he will not hate me too much when he finds out."

"Then you do not mean to see him and explain?"

"Explain?" she answered bitterly. "How can I explain my marrying a man I have grown to despise? No, I shall not go to him, nor must you. Nothing will change my mind now – I will be Ralph's wife."

Baton Rouge was too much like New Orleans to be of interest to Babette and she spent the long days of the honeymoon mostly in her room, venturing downstairs only for dinner or a theatre engagement with Ralph. At first he was quite attentive to her until he realised she was keeping to her word and had no intention of sleeping with him, then his attitude changed. He drank incessantly and began using violent language before her and in front of the hotel staff, and seemed to take delight in abusing her publicly. After he had twice returned blind drunk to their rooms, Babette locked the bedroom door for the last evening and when a maid brought breakfast the following morning, Ralph was snoring loudly on the couch.

After a heavy drinking session Babette found he was always sullen and irritable. He was no exception the morning they caught the boat home, and reverted to his favourite pastime at the gaming tables the moment they were on board, aided by one of the many heavily made-up hostesses who had caught his eye.

Babette wandered on deck, eager for the first glimpse of New Orleans. The day was overcast and humid, just like her wedding day. Her blue eyes clouded abruptly. The service in the small church on the Place Picard, Ralph's moist mouth brushing her forehead afterwards, the carriage drive to the waiting boat, they might have happened in a dream.

Was she really married to Ralph Weldon, trapped for the rest of her life, to be sworn at – humiliated at every turn, while her whole being cried out for love – a love denied her? She sighed deeply. No, she had denied it. She had chosen the way she must go. There was no turning back. She had looked for him as she came out of the church, hoping against hope that she would glimpse his tall figure among the onlookers, but she searched the sea of faces in vain and had climbed into the carriage near to tears.

Her mysterious lover was Ralph's choice topic of conversation whenever he favoured her with his presence. Sometimes she protested, but usually she allowed his sarcastic remarks to pass over her head, too unhappy to argue. Grant Tyler was never far from her thoughts, he filled them as she walked down the gangplank on her husband's arm. His sunburnt face hovered before her, those dark eyes that could not hide the desire he felt for her. Would it still linger now she was another man's wife? If only she had not promised never to make further contact with him, he might have listened to her explanation.

But deep in her heart, she was unsure. Explanations, excuses, they were all the same. She had placed her family's name and honour before her love for him – nothing could change that. What had he thought on reading of her intended marriage in the two most prominent newspapers? She knew he had seen it, otherwise he would have come for her as he promised.

A carriage waited in the roadway; Babette saw a familiar figure beside it and, leaving Ralph's side, ran to greet her brother.

"Am I to believe you are glad to see me?" Louis asked, with a smile, disengaging himself, after a long while, from her clinging embrace.

"Oh I am, I am," she breathed. "How are you? You look in the best of health, much better than a week ago. Why is Papa not here? Is he ill?"

Louis regarded her with a deepening frown. "Babette, how you do prattle on. I've never heard the like of it, and you're trembling. Somehow I anticipated the blushing bride still to be blushing." He glanced up and met Ralph's frosty stare. "Well – perhaps not under the circumstances. Into the carriage with you. I trust you both had an enjoyable stay in Baton Rouge; father has decided to throw a party to celebrate your homecoming."

"A party." A glow stole into Babette's pale cheeks. "Oh, how sweet of him."

"He might have discussed it with me first," Ralph said ungraciously.

"Etienne St. Clair is still master in his own house," Louis snapped, "even though you have now installed yourself in it."

Babette looked from one to the other in puzzlement. "What do you mean, Louis?"

"Ralph has sold his house," her brother answered in a more controlled tone of voice. "You are to live with us – Marguerite also."

"Your sister too," Babette gasped, staring at her husband. "But why? Could we not find a place of our own?"

Something glinted in Ralph's eyes which made her shudder. He was enjoying every moment of her discomfort.

"You were not so eager to be alone with me on our honeymoon, my dear, why the sudden change? This is a perfect arrangement. It will enable your father and me to work in close harmony."

Babette looked at him in dismay. To keep her father beneath his thumb, that was the real reason. She had little doubt his sister was to be her watchdog, making sure she behaved as propriety decreed a married woman should.

Marguerite Weldon came out to greet them as the carriage turned into the driveway. Babette tried hard not to look into her hard grey eyes, so much like Ralph's, as she stepped down to the ground. She had never liked her, now they were to live under the same roof. It would be an impossible situation. Not even Louis could give her the consolation she so desperately needed at that moment, and she sank lower into the depths of misery. Immediately after lunch, she went upstairs to her room. Her brother followed later and found her sitting in the window seat, lost in thought. Sitting beside her he drew her head against his shoulder, and gently stroked her hair.

"Pauvre petite, what have I done to you?"

Babette's voice was muffled against his jacket. "He drank almost every night," she whispered. "At last I could stand it no longer and I locked him out of my room. He hammered so fiercely on the door I was afraid he would break it down. It was like a nightmare."

"Then I thank God you and I are under the same roof. He won't dare touch you now. His room and Marguerite's are at the back of the house. I thought you would want them to be as far away from you as possible."

"Merci, mon frère."

Louis tilted up her chin and smiled down at her with a sudden show of brightness. "Cheer up, tonight we shall drink away our sorrows. You must wear your most alluring gown, it will do wonders for your morale."

Babette moved away from him, searching his face as she asked him softly, "Have you seen him?" She had no need to mention a name. A nerve twitched at the corner of Louis' mouth and she knew he had.

"I go to Sans Souci regularly," he replied.

"I did not ask you that."

"Yes – I've seen him, as recently as last night. At the moment I owe Monsieur Tyler a very large sum of money."

"Never mind that, I'll give you whatever you need," Babette answered, a catch in her voice. "Tell me, how does he look?"

Louis' eyebrows drew together in a deep frown. "How should a man look when the girl he loves has married someone else?"

"Louis, that was cruel," she cried, clutching a hand against her breast. "Are you blaming me?"

"No, *ma petite,* myself. Monsieur Tyler is a proud man and you have sadly wounded his pride. He puts on a good front, looking fine to everyone but me. I know how it feels – the longing, the heartache which slowly dies and the love which can turn so easily into hate." His eyes met hers, deeply troubled. "He came to the wedding. He stood across the street from the church, moving out of sight when you and Ralph appeared."

Babette sat stunned. He had come, but he had hidden himself. No wonder she had looked for him in vain. Then he must still love her.

"You want to see him, don't you?" Louis asked.

"Very much, but I cannot break my promise to Ralph."

"Promise! It was made under duress, it means nothing." If only that was true, Babette thought sadly.

"No, Louis, I made it willingly, knowing full well what it entailed."

"I underestimated you, little sister," Louis replied admiringly, "but is it worth it? One false move or a look in the wrong direction and Ralph will take great pleasure in spreading my grisly secret all around the town. You will not be able to stand it. You are young and in love. Go to Grant Tyler while there is still time. Don't give him a chance to think of you in Ralph's arms – his lips on yours. Oh, I know it's not that way, but Monsieur Tyler is not so well informed. Can you not imagine how he must be feeling?"

"And me?" Babette demanded. "You forget I am involved too – and you and father. *Mon dieu!* Louis, don't reproach me for what I've done. I can't bear it." She jumped to her feet, her wide eyes mirroring the anguish raging inside her. "One half of me says I must stay and carry out my part of the bargain; the other half tells me to run to Grant, beg his forgiveness and pray it isn't too late for us to be happy together."

Louis rose, his face growing thoughtful.

"Don't worry your head about it tonight. Perhaps tomorrow the solution will prove simple. Rest for a while – I want you to look your best at the party. If I see Ralph or Marguerite prowling in this direction I will tell them you are not to be disturbed."

He kissed her lightly and left her alone.

The first guests began to arrive at the house just after seven, while Jemima was still brushing Babette's hair.

"You had better go downstairs now," Babette said, taking the brush from her. "I can manage."

"Lordy, but you look pretty tonight," the old Negress murmured as she stood back. "Who is it for, chile, your husband – father – or the other one?"

"The other one?" Babette echoed in a small voice. She should have known better than to try and hide any secrets from Jemima who had nursed her from the cradle. "I am a respectable married woman now. I would not dream of making myself look pretty for another man."

"Married you may be," Jemima returned, a hard look on her face, "but it's to the wrong man if you ask me!"

Babette replaced the brush on the dressing-table before her and stared into the mirror, her cheeks growing pale.

"I did not ask you, Jemima. Please go downstairs at once and tell the others I will be with them in a moment."

Jemima had not been gone five minutes before the door opened and Ralph entered the room. Babette could tell at once he had been drinking by the way he leant heavily on his ebony-tipped cane.

"Are you too drunk to knock before entering?" she asked coldly.

"You are my wife, you know," Ralph reminded her sneeringly.

"It is something I am not likely to forget. You will see to that."

Babette smoothed the folds of her dress away from her waist. It was in heavy yellow satin, a beautiful contrast against her dark hair, and the bright colour made her feel better. She became aware of her husband's close scrutiny and an icy hand clutched at her heart. He moved towards her, but halted as she took a step backwards and ran his tongue over dry lips.

"Not yet," he said thickly. "Not while the house is full of people."

"You would not dare touch me!" Babette forced her voice to be brave.

"No? I might – but there is no hurry. I have all the time in the world." He held open the door for her, his eyes on her white face. "Our guests are waiting, my dear."

Babette tried hard to grasp the gay atmosphere of the party, but as the evening wore on, she was plagued by a nagging headache which refused to go away.

"I am going to grow angry with you," Ralph said once when they were dancing. He held her tightly against him, his lips against her cheek. The reek of whisky about him nauseated her, but she dared not turn away. "You lack vitality. I suggest you pull yourself together before people begin to talk. I would not like that. Do you understand?"

Mutely she nodded and his eyes narrowed in cruel satisfaction. When the music ended they began to mingle with the guests, receiving their congratulations.

"My dear child, you look radiant," her father said, bestowing a kiss on her forehead.

"Thank you, father," Babette answered quietly, wishing Ralph would lessen the painful grip he had on her arm. "It was sweet of you to welcome us home this way."

"Nothing but the best for the St. Clair family, and the Weldons, from now on, eh, Etienne!" her husband asked meaningly. "Come, Babette – we have many more people waiting to speak with us."

He kept her by his side for over an hour, but although she played her part as hostess perfectly, for ever smiling, Babette moved and conversed almost mechanically, remembering neither faces nor names as they moved around the room. She could have wept openly with relief when Ralph left her to seek out an old acquaintance.

"A delightful evening," a woman murmured in her ear, "I wish you both every happiness."

Babette nodded and thanked her. Everyone was being terribly kind. If only they knew the agony of mind she was forced to endure.

At the height of the party she stole away unnoticed to the peace and quiet of her father's study. Reclining on the chaise-longue, she heard the grandfather clock in the hall strike eleven. Her thoughts immediately flew to Sans Souci. It would be crowded now, people from all parts of the town jostling each other at the tables. Excitement would be running high. Grant would most likely be wandering amongst his customers, perhaps dealing in a poker game, his dark eyes intent on the cards in his hands. Did he think of her sometimes?

With a sigh she rose to her feet. Her guests would miss her if she lingered too long and then Ralph's temper would be provoked. She wanted no unpleasant scene tonight, she felt too wretched.

A man was standing in the hall when she came out of the study, talking to the butler. Another late guest, she thought, and directed her steps towards the drawing room without a second glance.

"Good evening, Mrs. Weldon."

She whirled around with a startled gasp, clutching at the gilt stair rail for support. How often during the long-drawn-out days at Baton Rouge had she recalled to mind those quiet tones, believing she would never again hear them. Slowly, she raised her eyes to meet his, and instantly recoiled at the fury she encountered there. With deliberate slowness Grant Tyler moved towards her.

CHAPTER
FOUR

IT seemed an eternity before Babette finally found her voice. Grant stood before her making no attempt to open the conversation himself, even though he could see his unexpected appearance had completely astounded her.

"What are you doing here?" she managed to ask. Her voice was barely audible.

"I was invited to a party, Mrs. Weldon." In the depths of his dark eyes anger sparkled, a complete contrast to his dazzling smile, which had not misled her for an instant, and she was frightened. Why had he come? "You are Mrs. Weldon, I presume?" he said calmly.

'You know I am," Babette returned, a crimson flush stealing over her face.

"Know!" he echoed and his tone challenged hers. "What do I know? Did you come and tell me of your wedding? Did you send a note? Perhaps it was mislaid in transit, servants grow more careless every day. This I know to be true: you have lied and tricked me since our first meeting, so I would be grateful if you would not fall on my neck with apologies or excuses. And please don't faint," he added as she swayed unsteadily, "I have no wish to invent a tissue of lies to explain the incident to your friends."

"Listen to me, for one moment," she pleaded. "I can explain –"

"It's too late for explanations," he interrupted harshly. "I'm playing the game by your set of rules from now on, and I give you fair warning, you will rue the day you ever heard of Grant Tyler."

Babette stared at him disbelievingly. Had this cruel,

austere man held her in his arms and kissed her so ardently? He was incapable of any deep emotion, otherwise he could not talk this way.

"What do you intend to do?" she faltered.

Grant gazed down into her trembling features with merciless eyes. He was a stranger – frightening – ruthless.

"I shall be in the garden at midnight, why not ask me then, if you can drag yourself away from your adoring husband. Tell me, Blue-eyes, is he richer than a mere gambler?"

"That isn't fair," she answered, wincing at his use of her pet name. It brought back so many memories.

"Who said I'm playing fair!" he retorted. "By the way, congratulations on your marriage. I'm sure you will both be very happy, you are so evenly matched."

"Grant, please – don't torture me so," Babette pleaded.

The red stain receded from her cheeks, leaving them remarkably pale. Her eyes pleaded with him to be gentle until they could be alone later and she could explain, but there was no mercy in Grant's heart, only revenge.

"I have a great deal to teach you about torture, child," he answered. Babette could find no reply. In that moment she could only think of Madame Seraphin and her prediction. She had married a man she did not love – she had been wanted by another and known the pleasure of his kisses! Was this the time for heartaches?

Louis came out into the hall. "Monsieur Tyler, I'm glad you could come."

Babette watched amazed as he shook Grant by the hand. "You invited him?"

"I have long enjoyed the hospitality of Sans Souci." Louis answered. "I thought it time Monsieur Tyler paid us a visit." He smiled at her and in his smile she read the real reason. He had brought Grant to the house for her benefit, in the hope that she could straighten things out between them. Sadly she shook her head.

"It was a mistake," she said.

Grant regarded her, a deep frown furrowing his brows.

"The mistake was yours," he answered in soft Creole French. "Now, if you will excuse me –"

Babette clutched at her brother's arm, but before she could speak Marguerite came hurrying across to them, her eyes alight with excitement.

"And who was that?" she asked in obvious admiration, her gaze following Grant's tall figure as he made his way to the nearest waiter.

"Monsieur Tyler, who owns Sans Souci. The gambling house," Louis replied quietly.

"Really – I must meet him."

Babette watched her slip through the dancers to Grant's side and touch his arm. A moment later they were dancing, Marguerite gazing up into his face, utterly captivated. The smile on Grant's face made her turn away in agony.

"Another conquest for Marguerite," Louis said dryly, placing a comforting arm around Babette's shoulders. "He will be lucky to be free of her for the remainder of the evening. Your sister-in-law clings like a leech to any man who so much as smiles at her. I must admit, however, she is quite attractive."

"She is far too thin," Babette retorted scowling. "Her nose is too long and that red hair – it never looks tidy. Besides, she changes her lovers as often as her dresses. Oh, Louis! He could not fall in love with her! He loves me. I know it –"

"What about your earlier conversation?" Louis asked pointedly.

"You heard?"

"Most of it. I warned you he was a proud man. He feels bitter, he wants revenge. Be careful he does not hurt you, *ma petite*. He is capable of it, you know."

Babette's eyes grew sombre. "If he does it will be no more than I deserve. Where is Ralph?"

"By the window with Henry Waverley."

"I see him." Her eyes stole to the grandfather clock.

"It is not time yet," her brother murmured. "Come, dance

with me. When you go into the garden I will make sure no one follows you I promise."

Babette tried unsuccessfully to ignore Grant, who seemed to be dancing every dance with Marguerite and openly enjoying it. He was deliberately trying to goad her to anger, she decided, but she would not rise to the bait. It was only natural that he should want to hurt her and she must bear it, whatever the cost to her own foolish pride.

A few minutes after midnight she slipped discreetly through the french windows into the garden. The night air was refreshingly cool on her burning forehead. She was drawn to the trees at the bottom of the pathway by a familiar tinkling sound. Suspended on the lowest branch of the first tree she came to, she discovered a set of wind-bells dancing merrily in the breeze.

"Do you like them?" Grant asked, moving out of the shadows beside her. He was so close she felt his hand brush her arm as he reached out to touch the pieces of glass. She could not contain the tremor that ran through her body.

"How exquisite," she breathed. "My mother used to have some when I was very young. I forget what happened to them."

"They are my wedding present to you," he said quietly. "Hang them in your bedroom window – listen to them as you lie in bed and think of me. Wish I was beside you."

Joy flooded over Babette at his words. He still wanted her. She felt a rush of tears to her eyes and hastily put up a hand to brush them away. She had not lost him!

"Do you mean it?" she asked.

Without warning he pulled her roughly into his arms. His mouth on hers was passionately demanding – more so than it had ever been before and she felt a flicker of fear run through her. This was not the gentle man she had grown to love, this was the violent man her brother had told her to avoid; taking what he wanted when it suited him, answerable to no one but himself. For the space of a heartbeat she resisted him, then the will to fight vanished. Her hands locked behind his neck and her lips clung to his in complete surrender.

When at last he drew away, Babette looked at him with shining eyes.

"You don't hate me? Oh, Grant! If only you knew how I longed for you to kiss me again."

His hands fell away from her, reluctantly she thought, but his next words rudely shattered her ecstatic illusion.

"No, I don't hate you," he said slowly. "I despise you. Did you think I would come crawling back after one kiss? How little you know of me, Blue-eyes."

Babette's senses reeled. She stretched out a hand and caught his sleeve, but he brushed it aside.

"You came here to humiliate me," she said, horrified. "Do you mean to tell Ralph of our relationship?"

"Relationship!" A crooked smile touched his mouth. "I would not call it such – not yet!"

"Then why, why did you come here? What harm do you intend to do to me?"

"To you directly – none. I may force your hand from time to time if I think my plans are progressing too slowly."

Babette's mouth grew dry with terror. What devil possessed him? Where was the gentle man who had taken her to the Mardi Gras? The passionate man who had kissed her by the bayou and then apologised for his forward behaviour? She barely suppressed a shiver of fear as she looked into his hard, merciless features.

"What – plans?" she stammered.

Grant leaned nonchalantly against a tree trunk, his arms folded across his chest, a half-smile on his face. He was enjoying this moment of triumph.

"You belong to me, Blue-eyes, and I intend to have you. In time you'll be glad to come to me and I'll dictate the terms," he drawled.

"You are mad!" Babette's laugh bordered on hysteria. Grant's eyes gleamed as he heard it. She was afraid – his aim had been achieved.

"Your brother Louis owes me a great deal of money," he continued ruthlessly. "I shall see to it he continues to gamble heavily. I believe your husband, also, enjoys a flutter when he is not seeking feminine company on the Rue Gallatin." He watched her flinch and shot home the final thrust. "By the foulest methods I know, I'm going to ruin your husband, Mrs. Weldon, and anyone else who stands in my way. When I have, you'll come crawling to me!"

Loathing and disgust flooded over Babette. How could she have imagined she loved this inhuman monster?

"How could you kiss me so – so – the way you did if you despise me?" she blurted out. If one spark of affection remained in him there was a faint hope.

"My God! What a child you are! Do you think you are the only woman I kiss that way? There are certain occupants in a house on Gallatin that could set you straight on that point –"

Babette struck out at his smiling face, but the blow never connected, he moved too quickly and instead her hand struck the hard muscles on his forearm.

"Louis will kill you for this!"

"Are you going to tell him?" Grant asked, apparently amused. "I hope not, for his sake. In a way, I almost like him, it would be a shame if I had to kill him, wouldn't it? Why not inform your esteemed husband of my plans?"

"I will! I will!" she cried.

"Please do, and then I'll acquaint him with the true facts. How I refused to continue our love affair after your marriage; of your vow to get even with me at any cost. Who will he believe?" He straightened and bowed slightly in her direction. "Goodnight, Mrs. Weldon. Sleep well." He sauntered casually back towards the house, taking a cheroot from his pocket as he did so.

He heard a cry, no, it was more like a moan, as he reached the patio, and turned in time to see Babette crumple to the ground and lie still. His face was completely expressionless as he halted to light the cheroot, his eyes without compassion as they rested on the pathetic huddle on the pathway, a splash of yellow amid the dark green shrubbery and black shadows. Then he continued into the drawing room.

"I think Babette has need of you," he said, stopping beside Louis, and walked on before he could be questioned.

The hubbub of voices grew loud and excited. As he reached the hall, a white-faced girl rushed past him and ran upstairs. Gathering up his gloves and cane, Grant opened the front door and went out into the night without a backward glance.

"Are you sure you are better?" Louis asked for at least the fifth time. He had carried the unconscious form of his sister to her room and sat with her for almost an hour before her senses returned. Her pallor was alarming and he was loath to leave her. "I'll have Jemima come and stay beside you."

Babette rolled her head dazedly on the pillows. "No, Louis, please. I want to be alone – quite alone."

Still he hesitated. What had been said in the garden to bring about her distressed condition? She was not easily upset or frightened, yet Grant Tyler had achieved both in a very short space of time. "Is there nothing I can bring you? No one –"

Her eyes filled with tears. "No." Her voice was hardly audible.

It was not until some while later Babette realised the wind-bells had been brought into the room and were hanging in front of the open window. Her eyes widened and grew misty at the remembrance of Grant's words. "Listen to them as you lie in bed and think of me. Wish I was beside you." The breeze stirred them, and their soft, enchanting music was the last recollection she had before she fell asleep.

Grant Tyler was not a vindictive man. He was quick-tempered, inclined to use his fists before his tongue, and he had inherited a ruthless streak from his father, but he had never considered himself to be vindictive. That was why he could not understand the fierce desire for revenge possessing him. Was it because Babette had tricked him with a false declaration of love, or because he was growing soft – trusting a pair of big, blue eyes when a year, six months before, he would not have restrained the insatiable desire to make her belong to him? He had never taken an unwilling woman. He had found money, wine and soft words, in that order, nearly always gave him his own way. Never before had he wanted a woman clinging to him like a leech – yet he had wanted Babette. He still wanted her, even though she was another man's wife, with a passion that considerably alarmed him. As the days passed, he grew more and more embittered at the thought of her lying in another man's arms.

For the third morning in succession he stood by the bedroom window watching the cold, grey light of dawn creep across the sky.

"Come in," he said, in answer to a knock on the door. His manservant, Sam, entered carrying a breakfast tray.

"I heard you moving around, Massa Grant; thought you might be feeling hungry. There's black coffee too."

"And why should I need black coffee?" Grant asked humourlessly.

Sam did not reply. Instead he slowly looked around the room, at the untouched bed, the half-empty bottle of brandy on a nearby table, the smouldering stub of a cheroot in a full ashtray. Grant followed his gaze, his dark eyes thoughtful.

"How many men would be needed to work the old plantation, Sam?"

"Fifty – maybe sixty. It needs a lot of work."

"But it could be done with fifty men?"

"Yes, sir!" The Negro's face broke into a beaming smile. "We goin' into the cotton business, Massa Grant?"

"Yes, Sam, we are. When St. Clair arrives tonight, bring him upstairs. I want to talk to him."

Grant dismissed him and began to dress, an idea forming in his brain.

That evening an apprehensive Louis St. Clair was shown into the study where Grant was reading.

"If it's about last night's I.O.U.s –" Louis began.

"Sit down," Grant interrupted quietly, waving him to a chair. "Cigar?"

"No."

Grant lit one himself and sat back in his chair, crossing his long legs before him.

"Can you repay the money you owe?" he asked at length.

Louis licked his lips nervously. "Given time."

"How much?"

"A month."

"Too long. What do you know about the running of a plantation, St. Clair?"

Louis looked astonished.

"I am not an authority, nor am I ignorant. The family used to own and raise cotton many years ago."

Grant drew deeply on his cigar.

"I want an overseer for my fields – someone I can trust completely. Regardless of the rest of your family, I think you are trustworthy. Anyway, it is a chance I'm willing to take."

Louis stiffened at the hidden reference to Babette. If only he had not promised her to remain silent he could have spoken on her behalf.

"Well?" Grant rose impatiently, staring down at him with hard eyes. "I'm a busy man, St. Clair. Do you agree?"

"I need time –"

"Three days. At the end of which I expect you to agree or pay your debt."

"I can't find the money in so short a time," Louis protested. "What game are you playing? Why have you changed towards Babette?"

A cold mask settled over Grant's face at the mention of her name. "That is hardly your concern."

Louis rose, measured his chances against the other man if it came to a fight and turned away, paling.

"I need a drink."

"On the table, help yourself."

Grant watched him pour a drink with an unsteady hand, splashing some on to the highly polished table. His lip curled in disgust, but he said nothing.

"What would I have to do?" Louis asked. A glass of whisky restored his courage. He poured another. "I mean if I accept?"

"I will provide the funds, and you will find me fifty good men to work the fields and see some kind of accommodation is provided for them."

"Slave prices are high."

Crossing to the large mahogany desk along one wall, Grant took a leather pouch from a drawer and tossed it on to the table.

"This will be more than enough."

Louis weighed it in his hand, staring at him intently. "I could go far on this kind of money," he said meaningly.

"I should find you, wherever you were," Grant answered, and by his tone the other man knew he meant it. He wondered if anyone had ever got the better of this unpredictable man. He suddenly thought of his sister and was sure that behind this strange offer was a scheme to get even with her – but how? Only by agreeing could he find out.

"Very well, Monsieur Tyler. I accept your offer," he said and held out his hand.

After a moment Grant reached out and clasped it.

Grant was in excellent spirits when he descended to the lower floor some time later and mingled with the clientele. He had not expected Louis to give in so easily. The fact that he had was a booster to his morale. Perhaps, after all, Lady Luck was on his side.

He had fallen into the habit of going to his study just after two every morning and Sam would bring him brandy and coffee. He was rarely disturbed at such an hour, and was mildly annoyed when his perusal of an interesting book was disturbed by Sam's face peering round the door.

"Lady to see you, Massa Grant."

"I wasn't aware I knew any," he replied dryly, but his

heart missed a beat. "Well, don't keep the lady waiting. Bring her in."

The woman who entered was not petite and black-haired as he expected; instead she was tall and over-dressed. Dyed yellow hair made a vulgar contrast against a low-cut dress which revealed more of her than was modest in society. Her painted face broke into a smile on seeing him.

"Hello, Grant. I thought there was only one Grant Tyler in the world – only one who would own a gambling house like this, anyway."

The years rolled back from Grant's memory. He chuckled and completely shocked Sam by moving forward and kissing her.

"Rachel! I don't believe it! After all this time! How long? Five years – no, six nearly. This has really made my evening. Sam, find some champagne. Have you eaten?" he asked the woman.

"Earlier. The champagne will be fine alone."

"Well!" Grant wheeled on Sam, grinning broadly. "What are you waiting for?"

"He's obviously not used to seeing someone like me in such a high-class establishment," Rachel said in an odd tone. "Perhaps I shouldn't have come – I might be bad for business."

"Nonsense. The girl I used to know was the main attraction." Grant took her cloak and gloves and seated her in a chair. "What will you have to drink? Sherry? Brandy?"

"Has it been that long?"

"Scotch – neat," Grant murmured. "Here – try this."

After a moment she looked up. "It tastes like the best in New Orleans. You really must be someone now!"

Grant did not miss the note of weariness in her tone, and wondered what had happened to age her so. The heavy make-up could not hide the deep lines at the corners of her eyes and mouth; lines which had not existed when he had known her. Rachel Sears – the toast of any Mississippi saloon or riverboat, her love of good living exceeded only by her love of money. They had been a team in those days, working the gaming tables on the river steamers. Before that it had been Jefferson City and St. Louis – one saloon and gambling house after another.

"When did you arrive?" he asked.

"A week ago."

"So long! Why haven't you come to see me before?"

A wry smile touched Rachel's lips. "You move in high circles, lover." She drawled the last word in her slow Southern manner and Grant had to laugh.

"Easy on the 'lover', Rachel, this isn't St. Louis. You still haven't answered me."

"Look at me. I don't fit in here and I wasn't sure of my reception. The company you keep is a little out of my class. I don't mind the men, but their fancy women make me sick."

Grant replenished their empty glasses, wondering what her opinion of Babette would be, or Marguerite Weldon, with whom he had recently struck up an acquaintance.

"I agree with you on the latter point," he answered. "How's life been treating you?"

"Need you ask?" A pair of shrewd green eyes challenged him.

"Out of work?"

"No – I have a job, as a hostess on the other side of town."

"In one of Millie's houses?"

"Yes. Do you know her?"

"Everyone knows Millie, every man who seeks a woman to sleep with anyway."

"You haven't changed. Still loving and leaving 'em as always."

"You have a suspicious nature, I'm a reformed character," Grant said. "Take a look around you. Would I have all this if I was keeping a woman as well?"

Rachel's gaze wandered over the bookshelves lining the walls, the luxurious carpeting underfoot and so many other things. Often when times were hard he had talked of the day when he would be rich. She had never believed in his dreams.

Now he was proving how wrong she had been. It puzzled her to think there was not a woman somewhere in the background. He had always liked the company of a woman if only to talk to. Surely the splendour of his home and the money which poured into his pockets from the tables downstairs were more than enough attraction.

Rachel knew Grant well. Over the years she had gradually learned how his mind worked. She knew to continue along the subject of women would not be wise – at least not at the present time. For Grant Tyler to deny emphatically that there was a woman in his life, meant he was very much entangled – willingly or otherwise.

They sat together until a magnum bottle of champagne had been consumed. By then it was growing light and Sam informed them the last customer had gone home.

"Will you stay for breakfast?" Grant asked Rachel.

"Millie will have my hide if I do."

"Tell her you had a difficult client," he answered, and ordered breakfast for them both.

Rachel produced a mirror from her bag and began to fluff her hair into place.

"My God – I look a mess. Is there somewhere I can make myself look more presentable?"

Grant opened the door to his bedroom. "Be my guest."

He leaned against the wall, his arms folded, watching her meticulously repair her make-up. He had often done the self-same thing, only before it had been in the dingy back room of a hotel or over a saloon. Their luck had never been good.

"What are you thinking?" Rachel asked. She smoothed some rouge along her thin cheekbones, wishing she had a natural colour.

"I was wondering how a small house in town would appeal to you," Grant replied, and saw her eyes widen.

"Are you offering to set me up?"

"I have a job which might interest you."

Rachel laughed and rose to her feet.

"For a moment I thought you were offering me the position as first lady of Sans Souci. What do I have to do?"

"Be amusing to someone here in town."

"A man?"

"A wealthy one whose chief weakness is a pretty woman. He's an old customer of Millie's."

Rachel joined him at the breakfast table, her eyes thoughtful.

"You make it sound promising. Is he married?"

"Yes." Grant could not hide a tinge of bitterness in his voice and Rachel did not miss it. She tried an indirect approach.

"Is he a business rival?"

"You might call him that. The plain truth is, I want him ruined. You'd be paid well."

"In the old days you'd have settled it differently," Rachel said quietly.

Grant nodded. He had never resorted to such methods before – but then he had never been in love before either.

"This is New Orleans, Rachel, I'm playing by their set of rules. The game is dirtier, the stakes higher – the reward more satisfying. Can I count on you?"

"Just tell me what I have to do."

Babette was horrified when she heard her brother had accepted the position of overseer of Grant's plantation.

"Work for him!" she exclaimed. "Louis, you can't!"

Louis peered at her over the top of his paper and she was surprised to find he did not look in the least worried.

"It's a debt of honour, *ma petite*, it must be paid. It's also a chance to find my feet again. For nearly three years I've gambled and drunk incessantly. It could make a man of me."

"You sound almost – pleased."

"Now I come to think of it, I am."

"But he's humiliating you. Imagine how people will talk. You, working for Grant Tyler. I will not let you do it."

"For once I am going to stand by the decision I made,"

Louis replied with unusual sternness. "Because of me you are married to Ralph. Not a very bright future, is it? Monsieur Tyler believes you are a scheming adventuress who preferred a rich husband to a loving one, also indirectly because of me." He shook his head slowly. "No, Babette, this time you will not take my part and that's my final word on it."

It may be yours, Babette thought determinedly as he returned to his paper, but not mine.

Both Ralph and Marguerite breakfasted in their rooms. It was easy for Babette to slip out of the house unnoticed not long afterwards. She made her way across the town, walking quickly, nervously, clutching a small black moiré bag in both hands.

The jeweller in the tiny shop in a dingy side street stared at her curiously when she produced her precious collection of jewellery, and studied it at great length. Eventually he offered her less than half the amount she asked and she could not raise the price higher. She was in the hallway when Louis came downstairs that evening.

"Are you going out?" he enquired.

"I am coming with you. Ralph has gone off somewhere and Marguerite is in her room with a headache. I feel in need of cheerful companions for the evening. Perhaps Lady Luck will smile on you and then there will be no need for you to work for Grant Tyler."

"Do you intend to see him?"

Babette avoided his gaze. "No, I do not," she lied, with wildly beating heart.

Her brother nodded and did not question her further.

Sans Souci was not so crowded as on the occasion of her first visit and she could see at once Grant Tyler was not at any of the tables. Patiently she stayed beside Louis, praying that his luck would change, thereby relieving her of the odious task before her. She did not see Grant come into the room, but suddenly she became aware of someone standing a few feet away from her and looked up. After the first brief shock

of seeing him again, she fought down the panic rising inside
her and even managed a rather aloof smile. It acknowledged
his presence – nothing more. He ignored her and sauntered
across to where Louis sat.

"Will you not join us, Monsieur Tyler?" Louis asked,
glancing up at him.

"My pleasure." Grant sat down in the vacant chair, conscious of Babette's eyes on him.

She stood a little to one side of him, watching his slim
hands dealing the cards. Fingers so quick and supple could
easily slip a card undetected from the bottom of the deck, she
thought.

Awaiting his turn, Grant had time to study her. Was it only
three weeks since their last meeting? She looked older and
very tired. The dark hair was swept high on to her head and
secured with jewelled combs, emphasising the pale, elfin
face. The blue dress she wore did more than justice to her
trim figure. He felt a surge of anger run through him as she
avoided his eyes.

"Your card, Monsieur."

Louis' voice was mildly reproving and Grant realised his
observation had carried him away. His concentration
returned once more to the game, but often he glanced up at
her, and watched her expression grow more and more
apprehensive as the stakes rose higher. Her brother was
losing heavily, threatening each time to play only one more
game, but as the evening wore on he still continued.

Babette was reaching a point of desperation. She watched
her brother push the last of his chips into the centre of the
table, and caught a glimpse of satisfaction in Grant's eyes. It
was a deliberate attempt to ensnare Louis so deeply in debt
that he would have to accept the job of overseer.

"Louis –" She put out a hand, a very shaky hand, and
touched his shoulder. "Louis – I feel most strange." She
swayed forward, eyes closed. Someone caught and steadied
her. A firm arm went around her shoulders.

"Perhaps you had better take her outside, St. Clair."

Grant's voice sounded close by her ear. Babette knew it was he who held her, although she dared not open her eyes. She leant heavily against him, passing a hand across her eyes.

"If I could lie down for a moment," she murmured.

"My sister has not been at all well these last few weeks, Monsieur Tyler," Louis said quietly. "This is her first evening out since leaving her bed."

"Then she shall rest upstairs until she is feeling better," Grant broke in. "Can you walk, Mrs. Weldon?"

Slowly Babette nodded, still not daring to look into his face.

"Good – there's no need for you to trouble yourself, St. Clair," he added as Louis rose. "My housekeeper will take good care of her."

Louis hesitated, then Babette raised her head and glanced at him, her eyes asking him to stay where he was. So that was it, he mused, his anxiety melting. She wanted to be alone with her lover. He resumed his seat as Grant helped her from the room.

The moment Grant and Babette were in the upstairs drawing room, hidden from the curious eyes which had followed their departure, his concerned pose dropped from him like a cloak. Closing the door behind them, he propelled Babette firmly to the nearest chair and pushed her into it, demanding coldly,

"And what reason have you for wanting to be alone with me?"

She knew it was useless to pretend otherwise and did not try. She was not dealing with a fool, but a clever, ruthless man.

Somehow she forced her voice to be calm. "I wanted to give you these." She pulled a jewel case from her bag and held it out to him. "They should cover Louis' gambling debts. I tried to sell them this afternoon, but the miserable little man I took them to would not give me a fair price."

Grant sorted methodically through the assortment. "Very nice – expensive too, but not enough."

"Not enough!" Babette gasped, horrified. "You are lying. The emeralds alone should cover half of the amount."

Grant closed the case with a loud snap and dropped it into her lap.

"I have no use for them. You forget I should have to sell them also. The price I might get would certainly be half of their true value and considerably less than your brother owes me. Besides, he's going to work it off."

He relaxed down on to the couch, watching her, a smile tugging at the corners of his mouth. "He's to be my overseer."

"Your lackey, you mean!" she cried angrily. "I won't let you do it."

Grant's face hardened.

"You have no say in the matter." Picking up the jewellery, he returned it to her evening bag.

Babette rose from her chair and stood before him. She was so pale he began to wonder if she might faint after all. "If it's revenge you want, take it out on me, not Louis, he's had enough unhappiness in his life."

"Tell me more, it sounds quite intriguing."

"Now you are laughing at me." The mockery in his voice stung her. She had come prepared to beg if necessary; now she found it impossible.

"It's revenge you want, I saw it on your face downstairs, but why Louis?"

"I'll tell you why," Grant answered. "Sit down, you may feel you need the support of something beneath you before I've finished."

White-faced, she stumbled backwards into the chair, her eyes riveted on him.

"My plans are progressing better than I anticipated," Grant said, reaching out to the decanter on the table beside him. "Will you take a little stimulant?" She shook her head. He shrugged and continued. "My main object, as you know, is you."

Babette drew in her breath, but did not speak.

"There are two obstacles in my path," Grant went on relentlessly, "your brother and your husband, but I anticipate trouble from neither of them. Louis owes me a great deal of money, and as from last night he's also one of my employees. Until he can find his way out of these situations he's in no position to challenge anything I do."

As if in a dream Babette heard herself asking, "And Ralph – my husband?"

Amusement flickered in the depths of Grant's eyes. "He's no problem."

"He is highly respected in New Orleans," she said slowly. "You cannot intimidate him as easily as Louis, nor discredit him."

"Could I not?" She did not like his confident tone. How much did he know of Ralph's frequent visits to the other side of the town?

"What do you mean?"

"Simply this," Grant answered. "In the past I've discovered the extent of a man's influence depends on the money backing him. Ralph Weldon is not poor, not with your dowry safely in his possession and a half interest in your father's shipping line. But then neither am I, although I admit purchasing your father's half of the line did cost me more than I anticipated. He's a shrewd business man. I have the greatest respect for him." He stared solemnly into Babette's horror-stricken face. "Yes, Blue-eyes – I am now Ralph's partner."

"What will you gain by it?" she faltered.

"Eventually I shall buy him out and take over the line completely myself. Adding that to Sans Souci and the plantations, once they are in production again, I think I'll be in a position of advantage. Don't you agree?"

"Advantage to do what?" she asked in a hollow tone.

He chuckled. "Come now, don't be so naïve. I've told you once already, must I repeat it? I regard you as my property and I intend to have you."

CHAPTER
FIVE

GRANT'S composed manner sent a shiver of fear along
Babette's spine. He regarded her as his property and when he
said the words he sounded just like Ralph. Yet, no two men
had ever been so different – or were they? Grant had laughed
at the idea that she was the only woman in his life. Did he
follow Ralph's example and seek solace among the willing
feminine company in the less desirable parts of the town? She
shuddered to think he did. Not Grant, not the gentle man
who had held her in his arms and spoken of love.

Her face grew clouded. He was not always gentle, as she
had discovered the night of the party, and she had grown
afraid of the new man, the ruthless, mocking Grant Tyler
who faced her at this moment, cruelly taunting her. He
wanted revenge. There was nothing he would not do to
satisfy the craving and in the end he would claim her. Her
heart almost stopped beating as she looked up at him, trembling in every limb.

"You would not –" she hesitated, "could not take me
against my will!"

"No?" Grant's eyebrows rose quizzingly. It was a question, but also an answer and she realised nothing would deter
him, not even her unwillingness.

"I'm not so sure you will be unwilling," he said softly, and
the colour fled from her cheeks. Had she given herself away?
No, it was impossible. She had said nothing to give him any
indication her love for him still remained.

"If you do this thing, I shall hate you!" she answered
vehemently.

"Even when I'm rich!" Grant flung back. "I shall be richer

than Ralph, Blue-eyes, much richer. I think I'll be able to tempt you."

"If you were the last man on earth I should resist you," she said and saw the disbelief in his eyes. You are right, she thought miserably, you will be able to tempt me. Not with money or jewels or a fine house, but with yourself. A look – a caress – a soft endearment.

She closed her eyes, shutting out his piercing gaze. How could she fight him when she loved him so? Her whole being ached for him to teach her, hold her close against him. Only the knowledge that he was using her as an instrument of revenge kept her from blurting out the truth about her marriage, confessing that Ralph had never made love to her; that they were strangers, and of the secret which had prompted her to such hasty action.

"I don't suppose Ralph knows of your transactions with my father?"

"No. Do you intend to tell him?"

"Yes, tonight." She turned away towards the door. In two long strides Grant was before her, one hand on the elaborate silver handle, the other closing around her waist like a vice.

"It will do you no good to go to him and make a scene. It will only cause you great embarrassment," he said.

"Let me go, Monsieur Tyler."

"In a moment. First I want to show you something which may change your mind."

He led her out on to the landing overlooking the gambling room and moved along it until the roulette table was directly in their line of vision.

"Look carefully," Grant ordered. "Tell me who you see there."

Babette looked. He felt her stiffen as she caught sight of her husband, leaning over the table. A heavily made-up blonde girl was clinging possessively to his arm. That did not surprise her, but his presence at Sans Souci did, and the panic rising inside her bordered on hysteria. He would lose, she knew he would – fate was on Grant Tyler's side.

"You are not human," she breathed.

Grant made no answer, but turned back into the drawing room. She stumbled after him, a shrill shriek of laughter from Ralph's companion following her into the room.

"Sit down," he said quietly.

Almost on the point of collapse, she fell into a chair.

Neither Grant nor Babette spoke for a long time. She sat in a stunned silene, aware of him moving around the room, yet not seeing him. She felt exceedingly faint.

"Drink this."

He pressed a glass into her hands. She swallowed a little of the contents, grimaced at the raw liquor and put it to one side.

"Was he winning?" she asked at length.

"At the moment, yes, but he's over confident. Soon he'll grow careless and begin to lose."

Babette made one final attempt to change his mind.

"Is there nothing I can say to stop you?"

He shook his head gravely. "Nothing. You played me for a fool. Now you must face the consequences."

"But I didn't!" she cried out tremulously, her blue eyes wide with anguish. Looking into them, Grant had to force himself to stay where he was. "I had to marry Ralph."

"Of course, I quite understand. He's influential – wealthy – a good family match –"

"No! No – I had to!"

"Why?"

She fell silent. He took a step towards her and stood beside the chair, hands on hips. "There's only one way to change my mind, tell me why you married Weldon?"

Bright tears glistened in her eyes.

"I can't. Please don't ask me. It's the one thing I can't divulge."

"Then there's nothing left to say."

"But there is." Babette rose to her feet, her chin tilting proudly. "Think what you like about me – it's no longer of importance, but if you try to drag Ralph or Louis through the mud, I'll fight you every inch of the way."

"I didn't expect an easy victory," Grant returned. "However, there's very little you can do. Louis is repaying a debt of honour. Ralph, he'll come to heel over a business transaction I have in mind. Telling one or both of them of my intentions will not help you. It will only add to your own troubles and it will certainly not help them."

"All this because your pride has been hurt," Babette said scornfully.

His jaw tightened, but he did not fly into a temper as she expected and his confident pose unnerved her more than anything.

"Pride is all I have left," he answered coldly. "You left me little else. Weldon has nothing against me. I doubt if you could convince him I was out to ruin him. He likes it here, the chance to play with high stakes, the feminine company provided."

Babette rounded on him suspiciously.

"Provided!" she echoed.

"Of course," Grant said, with a tight smile. "Rachel is in my employ. She will do anything for money, not that she's different from anyone else. You are in a dilemma, Blue-eyes, unable to turn to either husband or brother."

"Ralph will listen to me." Babette's voice was very low. "You forget I am a woman."

Grant's eyes narrowed sharply, anger glinting in their depths. She drew in her breath sharply. Had she gone too far?

"By all means try, my dear. I shall be forced to inform him of your scandalous behaviour at the Mardi Gras. Pretending to be a gypsy girl so that you could meet your lover, not once but three times!" He paused, the anger fading. "I could elaborate quite a bit, as I've said before. In fact I could make it quite sordid."

Sick at heart, Babette stumbled across the room towards the door.

"One moment!" Grant moved in front of her, barring the way. "Are you so anxious to leave my company?"

"Please let me pass."

He stood firm, staring down at her. "I'll be waiting for you at the old plantation house at sun-up."

"I will not come," she gasped. "You are mad to suggest such a thing."

The sardonic smile she hated returned to his face. "You will do as I say. If you want to retrieve Louis' I.O.U.s."

Was she hearing aright? Babette wondered dazedly. He was offering to return them to her.

"How do I know you will bring them?"

Grant matched her scornful stare.

"My word is my bond," he answered cuttingly. "Be there at sun-up, alone."

Without waiting for her answer he opened the door and ushered her out. Louis was waiting for them at the bottom of the staircase, his face wreathed in smiles.

"You have brought me luck, *mignonne*," he said, drawing her to him. "I have won continually all evening."

"Oh, Louis, I am glad."

"Congratulations," Grant said dryly.

"And now, Monsieur Tyler — a little matter of settling some of my debts to you."

Babette caught the glance Grant directed at her, and her grasp tightened on her brother's arm.

"Louis, I would like to go straight home. Could it not wait —"

He looked down at her concernedly.

"Of course — I will see you tomorrow night, Monsieur, if you agree."

"At your convenience," Grant answered.

"Did you know Ralph was at Sans Souci tonight?" Louis asked as their carriage rolled homewards.

"Yes, as a matter of fact, I did," she answered.

Her brother gave a soft chuckle. "Babette, you never cease to amaze me. Your fainting act killed two birds with one stone, enabling you to be alone with Monsieur Tyler and out of sight of Ralph.''

Babette said nothing and allowed him to chatter on until the house was reached, successfully evading the answering of any questions concerning her present relationship with Grant Tyler. Feigning a headache, she went straight upstairs to her room and locked the door behind her. While she was undressing, a breeze from the open window stirred the wind-bells, bringing to mind what she had to do next morning. What foolishness had prompted her to agree to the meeting? He would not keep his word to bring the damning I.O.U.s and she would be forced deeper into deception.

From the depths of the large chest of drawers in one corner of the room, she took a tiny Derringer and thrust it deep into the pocket of her riding jacket. Here at least was some protection.

Contrary to her threats, Babette made no attempt to see Ralph and explain the awkward situation she found herself in. She heard him come in next morning as she was about to get up, knowing full well by the sound of his dragging footsteps that he was drunk. The handle of her door turned slowly, and she heard a muttered oath as he discovered it was locked and staggered on past to his own room.

Trembling violently, she began to dress. How could she ask his help, advice even. To place herself in his debt would be the same as placing herself at his mercy. She knew what his price would be and it was too high. Grant Tyler was demanding the same thing, yet she was not seized with the same awful feeling of revulsion when comparing the two men. How could she when she still loved one of them?

None of the house servants were awake as she slipped silently down the stairs, unbolted the front door and made her way around the back of the house to the stables. The small Negro stable-boy looked at her as if she had taken leave of her senses when she roused him from a sound sleep and ordered him to saddle her bay mare. She then told him to go back to sleep, threatening him with a whipping if he told anyone she had gone out. She had never laid a finger on any of the servants and would not have carried out her threat, but it was enough to send the boy scuttling back to his bed of straw, suitably cowed.

The sun was just breaking through the blue-black hue of clouds as she urged the horse into a wild gallop past Sans Souci. The wind stung her cheeks, but she did not slow down until she reined-in before the derelict plantation house. As before, Grant was waiting for her, this time mounted on a superb black stallion. He was a good judge of horseflesh, she thought begrudgingly, and wondered if she was meant to be impressed. He wore dark riding breeches and a dazzling white silk shirt, open at the neck, an attractive contrast against his sunburnt skin.

Stiffly she moved her horse to his side, steeling herself to remember that this man meant her only harm and humiliation. Her feelings for him had not changed, but he no longer loved her. To harbour thoughts of regaining his affection could only have disastrous results.

"I am here," she said coldly. "Give me what I came for and let me go."

"In a moment," he answered quietly. "Would you care to take a look over the fields? I fancy they have changed since you were here last."

Colour flamed into Babette's cheeks at the memory of her last visit here with him. They had declared their love and kissed as lovers do, an experience she had not found as distasteful as she feared. Now they were strangers – enemies.

"Do I have a choice?" she asked, trying to retain her rapidly diminishing dignity.

"You may leave if you wish – without the I.O.U.s."

"And if I come with you?" What choice had she?

"I shall give them to you afterwards."

She lifted her shoulders in a slight shrug – a gesture of submission.

His smile grew. Motioning her to ride beside him, he wheeled his horse about and cantered off towards the plantation. After a brief moment of hesitation, Babette followed, not knowing what to expect and hoping she would have enough self control to remain aloof and disinterested in whatever he wanted to show her.

However, she was not prepared for the scene which met her eyes when they rode down on to the narrow pathway bordering the fields.

The land was no longer in a state of neglect. Weeds, fallen tree-trunks and all debris had been cleared. Long well-cared-for rows of fleecy white cotton faced her, and moving along them, more than thirty or forty coloured people, men and women. She caught the soft sound of singing. It was reminiscent of childhood days, and her heart ached for those times when her mind had been free of troubles. Grant sat back in the saddle to light a cheroot, his dark eyes studying her thoughtfully, waiting for her reaction now she had discovered he was no longer just a gambler. Once the plantations were in full production he would be among the first three most wealthy and influential men in New Orleans.

Babette allowed her gaze to dwell on the rolling acres before her. At length she said, "Is this why you wanted Louis to work for you?"

Grant nodded. "I needed someone with experience. I believe your family once owned a similar plantation."

"Many years ago, now," Babette answered. "It was destroyed in a fire. We were unable to salvage anything of value."

Grant leaned towards her in interest. "Go on."

"There is nothing more to tell. We moved to New Orleans, that's all."

"And your father turned to the shipping line?"

"He already owned it," Babette said icily. "I'm surprised you haven't made it your business to check into our background. After the fire he was forced to take on a partner."

"Ralph Weldon?"

"Yes. Ralph promised to sell out once father was on his feet again." Her voice grew bitter. "He didn't mean it, of course. In time he hoped to take over the line completely."

"But he settled for you instead," Grant mocked.

"No, it's still his intention to do so – at least it was." She looked at him curiously. "Father hasn't told him you now own his half. Why?"

"I asked him not to. I'm asking you to keep silent also."

"Asking or telling?" she demanded.

Grant smiled into her indignant features, not in the least perturbed by the anger sparkling in her sapphire blue eyes.

"Which would you prefer? I could threaten you into silence, but I prefer to think you are sensible enough to keep quiet without such measures."

"As usual, I have little alternative," she answered and he heard a note of weariness in her tone. It gave him great satisfaction to know that she was at last acknowledging he had the upper hand.

They were nearing the ruins of the house. Grant reined in and stared at it thoughtfully.

"I'm having this place rebuilt," he said at length, and smiled at the look of startled amazement on Babette's face. "The idea was yours in the first place, if you remember."

"Surely Sans Souci suffices for your needs," she replied, trying to appear uninterested What was all this leading up to? It both puzzled and frightened her.

"True, it does, at the moment, but later on, when we are together, Sans Souci will be too crowded. When I make love I prefer it to be to an audience of one."

Babette reeled back in the saddle, a hand against her mouth. He turned to stare at her with steely eyes.

"Why do you look surprised? You know I mean to have you."

"Is it your intention to set me up in that house as – as your mistress?"

A crooked smile touched Grant's mouth.

"What else?" he flung back carelessly.

Fierce colour flooded into her cheeks, then receded leaving her a deathly pale. She clutched tightly at the pommel of

her saddle, as if without its support she might tumble headlong to the ground.

"Is that all you want from me?" Her voice was hardly
audible.

Grant steeled himself against the anguish mirrored in her
eyes. This was another innocent act, meant to deter him from
his purpose. Coldly he said, "You have little else to offer,
Mrs. Weldon."

Babette began to tremble. She was about to make a desperate attempt to save those near to her. Ralph was of no
consequence, but her father and brother had to be spared this
man's revenge, even if she paid dearly for it.

"If I come to you – of my own free will – tonight, or
whenever you wish, would you leave my family alone? They
have done you no harm. It's me you want to hurt, so take me
and have your revenge."

Her words shattered Grant. Never in the wildest throes of
his imagination had he thought she might offer herself to
him. He allowed his gaze to wander insultingly over her, and
he was seized with a desire to lash at the face he had once
loved to caress. When he spoke his voice was like the sharp
crack of a whip – deadly, wounding.

"To think I respected you enough to keep my hands off
you. My God! You make me feel sick! No, Blue-eyes, you'll
not have it your own way. First I'll dispose of all opposition,
then I'll have you, and it won't be in secret, behind locked
doors. You'll come to me openly or I'll drag you through
New Orleans by your hair for everyone to see."

"You mean to disgrace me publicly," Babette whispered.
She was appalled by the lengths he meant to go to repair his
wounded pride.

"The gutter is too low for you," Grant snapped.

Babette cried out and slumped forward in the saddle,
overwhelmed with shame. She had offered herself to this
man – a man who did not hide the fact he had sought solace in
the unmentionable houses along Gallatin and elsewhere.

Something hard dug into her breast. Her hand touched the

cold steel of the Derringer in her pocket and she pulled it out into the open with a defiant gesture.

"You are not fit to live!" she cried.

Grant stared at the pistol with narrowed eyes. Another attempt, slightly more dramatic than before.

"Really, Blue-eyes! If you were to kill me, you'd have to find another lover. Why put yourself to so much trouble, they may be more particular than I am –"

Babette was not aware of her finger tightening around the trigger. Yet suddenly there was a loud report and Grant clapped his hand to his shoulder, emitting a grunt of pain. Before her horrifed eyes, blood began to trickle through his fingers, soaking the front of the silk shirt.

"I – I –" The words stuck in her throat. Paralysed with fear, she remained rooted in the saddle while he slid awkwardly to the ground.

Attracted by the shot, numerous workers started in their direction – some began to run. Panic surged through Babette like wildfire and with trembling hands she gathered her reins and wheeled about.

"Not so fast –"

Grant staggered towards her, a hand outstretched to detain her. She felt him catch the nearest stirrup and used her riding crop viciously on the mare's flank – something she had never done in her life before. Grant was flung to one side. She glimpsed his face, twisted with pain and fury as she galloped past, out of the plantation, towards home and safety. She did not – dared not – look back.

Louis came into his sister's room a few minutes after the dinner gong had sounded. Despite a whole afternoon of weeping, not a sign showed on Babette's face as she looked up at him.

"You saw Monsieur Tyler this morning?" Louis asked quietly.

"Yes – what of it?" She fought down the panic which threatened her composure.

"Did you shoot him?"

"I – shoot –" Babette feigned surprise so well he was deceived. He laid a comforting hand on her shoulder as she sank down on to a stool and covered her face with her hands.

"Forgive me, *mignonne*, it's obvious you know nothing of what has happened." He straightened, his eyes puzzled. "Even I am at a loss as to what actually took place."

Babette raised a stricken face to his. Then realising she was supposed to be ignorant of the facts, she asked, "When did this happen?"

"This morning, just after you had left him, apparently. I was on my way to the plantation when I heard the shot. By the time I arrived he was unconscious. I managed to get him back to the house and had his manservant go for a doctor." Begrudging admiration crept into his voice. "I've got to hand it to him, Babette – he's no coward. I was present while the bullet was extracted. It was in a damned awkward spot, smashed the bone in the shoulder and lodged behind it, yet he didn't utter a sound. Do you know I'm actually beginning to respect that man? Monsieur Tyler isn't laying charges against anyone, but God help the person when he's caught. It won't be pleasant for him."

"What makes you so sure it's a man?" Babette asked.

Louis smiled, idly toying with the wind-bells suspended before the open window.

"Monsieur Tyler said so. At least he said it was someone who had a grudge against him. Of course he meant a bad loser at Sans Souci."

"Of course," she echoed. So Grant had not confided in her brother!

Louis looked into her pale features with sudden compassion.

"The wound is not too serious, little one. Rest and quiet is all he needs." He longed to question her and learn why she had made a secret rendezvous with Grant Tyler. Had she at last decided to be sensible and go to him whenever possible? A brief meeting now and then would be better than years of unhappiness with Ralph. The mere thought of him touching her sickened him. He would fight tooth and nail to prevent it ever happening.

Dinner in the St. Clair house had become a rather sombre affair. Conversation was something rare. It was usually Marguerite who brought up the latest gossip with a malicious eagerness that made Babette's hatred of her grow each passing day. Or Ralph discussed business with Etienne St. Clair. There was an air of gloom whenever they all came together.

"I hear someone tried to kill the owner of Sans Souci today," Ralph remarked when they were all assembled in the drawing room.

Marguerite went a ghastly colour and almost dropped her glass of sherry.

"Grant!" Hastily she corrected herself. "Monsieur Tyler? It cannot be true."

Babette stood behind her in a stunned silence. How easily his first name had slipped out.

"It's true," Ralph answered. "A pity his assailant wasn't a better shot, he's one man I'd like to see dead." He rounded on his sister with a soft exclamation. "You appear distressed at the news. I was not aware you were intimately acquainted with him."

Marguerite gave a low amused laugh.

"Is it so hard for a man look at me?" she asked. "I'm not unattractive and he has shown interest in me." She stared at her brother challengingly. "I have dined with him several times. Should he ask me to do so again, I shall accept."

Ralph threw back his head and roared with laughter. The thought of Grant Tyler interested in his two-faced, conniving little sister was too funny for words. He did not notice Babette stumble blindly to a chair and sit down.

"By all means have your fun, dear sister," he mocked, "but don't come running to me when he throws you over. At my estimation you'll last no longer than a month; then when he finds out what a scheming cat you are, he'll turn to someone else."

"Ralph!" Marguerite sprang from her chair. "You would do well not to reproach me, I know too much about Rachel –" she broke off, casting a sneering glance at Babette. "You poor fool. You should have chosen your lover," she said and swept out of the room.

Babette shrank back in her chair. Rachel – the name was disturbingly familiar. It was the girl Grant had hired to keep her husband company and ensure he spent lavishly at the gaming tables. She was taking her work seriously.

"If you will excuse me, I think I will go to my room." Unsteadily she rose to her feet and bade goodnight to her father.

"Why not come with me to Sans Souci?' Louis asked. "A night out will do you good."

"No thank you, it will be far too crowded."

"Nun," Ralph growled, replenishing his empty glass. "That's what you're trying to be."

"If it's her wish, then it will be," Louis returned coldly. "You find your pleasures elsewhere – be satisfied."

Babette almost ran from the room. Daily Ralph was growing bolder. Soon, she feared, he might attempt to force his marriage rights and if he did, Louis would surely kill him.

An hour later she watched a carriage draw up outside the house. Marguerite and Ralph climbed into it and were driven away. When Louis came to say goodnight, he tried again to persuade her to accompany him, but she refused and went straight to bed.

Sleep was impossible. Babette lay listening to the sound of the wind-bells tinkling prettily in front of the open french windows, but tonight the sound of their music failed to soothe her troubled mind. She had tried to kill Grant Tyler – had tried and failed . . . The memory of the blood pouring from the wound in his shoulder, as he leapt towards her horse in a desperate attempt to prevent her riding off, was still uppermost in her mind. What would he have done to her if he had succeeded in making her stay? Yet had she really meant

to kill him? No – her one thought had been to retrieve Louis'
I.O.U.s by any means in her power. The Derringer had been
meant to frighten him – not harm him. How silly of her to
think such a man could be frightened by the sight of such a
weapon and held – not by a grim-faced adversary who meant
business, but a trembling, half-hysterical girl, trapped by her
own web of lies and deception.

Louis had said he was not badly hurt. That knowledge was
of little consolation. What would he do – how would he have
his revenge on her?

A shiver ran through her body and she pulled the bed-
clothes higher around her shoulders. Even though it was a
hot, sultry night, she was feeling uncomfortably cold. Fear!
Fear that Grant would somehow make her brother pay for
what she had done. He still had the I.O.U.s – in her haste to
flee she had completely forgotten them. It had all been for
nothing . . .

She had gone to him prepared to offer anything in return
for Louis' I.O.U.s – even herself. The shame which had
engulfed her when he had refused even that humiliating offer
would never be wiped from her mind. She had not meant to
pull the trigger even then, but his taunts had goaded her
beyond all reasoning . . .

How cold she was . . . perhaps if she rang for Jemima to
bring a glass of warm milk, that might help her to sleep. No,
all the servants would be in bed by now except Jason, who
had been ordered by Ralph to await his return – she would
close the windows and read for a while.

Climbing out of bed, Babette pulled a wrap around her
shivering body and then froze in terror as a shadow from
outside invaded the room . . . the unmistakable outline of a
man. He had come in through the back gate into the gardens
below and used the staircase which led up to her room – and
her room alone. She gave a shaky laugh and started towards
the window. Louis – of course, it had to be. He had lost again
at the tables and come back to her for solace . . . he would
keep her up half the night bemoaning his bad luck, but she

would not mind. Anything was better than being alone just now.

"Don't tell me, Louis . . . you are down to your last silver dollar," she said lightly.

"When I left him, he was winning – for a change," Grant said in a quiet tone as he stepped over the threshold. The window had closed behind him, trapping them in the same room together, before Babette realised what was happening. For a moment she stared at him unbelievingly, her wide eyes taking in the arm which hung limply at one side, the white bandages swathed high around his neck and clearly visible beneath the open neck of his shirt before lifting slowly to his set features.

"What . . . what are you doing here? Don't . . . don't come any closer or I will scream for help . . ."

"And rouse your father, who is no doubt sleeping soundly by now – or Jason? I am more than a match for either of them despite this useless arm for which I have you to thank," Grant returned bitterly.

She backed away in alarm as he stepped further into the room. He regarded her humourlessly for an instant, before dropping into the nearest chair. She realised he was exhausted. How had he come to the house? She had heard no carriage. It was almost half an hour's walk from Sans Souci unless he had taken the back paths through the bayou, and for a man in his condition, that was unthinkable, yet looking down at him slumped in the high-backed chair, she knew that was exactly what he had done.

He stared at her with a frown as she gathered the robe she wore close about her body. She expected some sarcastic comment, but instead he said:

"What's wrong, have you caught a chill? Too many early morning rides," he added, to dispel any idea he might be genuinely concerned, she thought.

"No – I was asleep – you frightened me." That was the truth. She had never experienced such fear in all her young life.

"If that's all I do tonight, then count yourself very lucky," Grant growled. "You need something to warm you – have you anything to drink up here?"

"Here?" Babette echoed. "This is my room, not one of your Gallatin women's places of entertainment. All hard liquor is kept in my father's study."

"I'm sure he will not object to us both sampling some of his best Bourbon – for medicinal purposes, of course."

"I – I cannot go downstairs," Babette said, aghast at such a suggestion. If she was seen – and with a bottle of Bourbon? There was no way she could answer the presence of this man in her room, and he knew it. He was being deliberately cruel . . . payment for the pain she had caused him, and he was in pain – she could see that now she had turned up the oil lamp. It was mirrored in the depths of his eyes, in the greyness of his cheeks.

"Perhaps you would prefer me to go, although I may not be as quiet . . ."

"No – no, stay here," Babette pleaded, starting forward and he relaxed back in his chair with a satisfied smile. "I will bring you what you want. Do not be so sure I will not arouse my father. You are not the only one who could concoct a convincing set of lies. I think my word would be accepted in preference to yours." She made a last desperate attempt to smash the confidence which radiated from him, threatening to subdue her into obedience.

"Do you really? Yes, perhaps you could with tears and a few innocent sighs, persuade people I had broken into your room. But why, Blue-eyes – why should I bother to seek you out instead of going to someone more, shall we say, accommodating? Someone I should pay well for her services? It needs only the slightest hint of suspicion to start the tongues wagging . . . what then? How will you walk down the street knowing what is being whispered about you behind those delicate lacy parasols? How will you live with the knowledge you have brought disgrace on the family name . . . and ruined Louis, your own brother?"

Babette reeled back from him until the edge of the chaise-longue gave her the support she so desperately needed. How could he know the memories his taunts had aroused? She had, through her own stupidity, hurt Louis once before. His life was already in ruins because she had failed to keep a promise . . .

"What – what would you do to him?" she whispered in an agony of suspense.

"What should I do? Without these I have no hold over him." Grant tossed a familiar wad of paper on to the table beside him. "I came to return these. If you remember, it was why I asked you to meet me – and unlike some people I can think of I am a man of my word. I think that at least deserves the courtesy of a drink."

Babette knew it was useless to argue further – or to fetch Jason. Perhaps if she gave him what he wanted he would leave as he had come, without anyone else being the wiser.

Feeling rather like a sneak-thief, she stole downstairs, took a bottle and a glass from the study and crept back upstairs. Grant had not moved from his chair, she noticed as she quietly closed the door after her. She was seized with another bout of shivering as she put both items down beside him.

"Pour yourself one," he ordered.

"Certainly not."

Uncorking the bottle by placing it between his knees and using his uninjured hand, he splashed a small amount into the glass and held it out to her with a look which defied argument.

"Humour me."

Babette had never taken spirits in all her twenty years and she coughed as the strong mature Bourbon slid down her throat, and thrust the glass back towards him. He filled it almost to the brim, drank a little and then put it to one side.

The wad of I.O.U.s on the table held Babette's attention. If she snatched them out of reach and then screamed . . .

"Take them." She could have hit him for the accurate way he read her thoughts. "I think now you realise I am capable of

doing – and going, exactly what and where I choose –
whenever it pleases me. If you remember that in the future,
we shall perhaps avoid scenes like this again. I am not accustomed to entering by the back door," he added, as if to imply
that every front door in New Orleans was open to him just for
the asking.

"And what price have you placed on them this time?" The
words stuck in her throat, but she forced them out. He was
out for revenge, but what form it would take eluded her. He
was a devil!

"You already know that."

"Then for pity's sake, why did you come here?" she cried.

"Why?" Reaching into an inside pocket Grant produced a
cheroot and slanted it between his lips. His match case was
held out towards her with a quiet order. "Light this for me –
you have made even the small task of lighting a cigar damned
awkward."

"I am not one of your . . . your women . . ." Was it the
Bourbon that made her suddenly so defiant? The gleam
which sprang to his eyes warned her that the remark had been
foolish.

Before she could guess his intentions, he was on his feet,
his good arm encircling her waist. Despite the hands she
braced against his chest she was drawn against him until his
mocking features were only inches away from hers.

"You will be whatever I want you to be, Blue-eyes. You
have no other choice. This morning you could have been free
of me – had you killed me, of course – but you failed, and I
promise you will never come close to getting another
chance."

And then his mouth was on hers, his kisses smothering her
frightened cries until Babette felt her senses reel. She felt
herself lifted and then borne backwards to be laid down on
the canopied bed where she had once lain awake and planned
a new life with this indestructible monster bent on destroying
her to avenge his wounded pride.

For a moment longer she was forced to endure his lips on

hers and then – just as she felt herself begin to respond – he had drawn back and his voice came to her out of the shadows as he moved back towards the windows, mocking that last moment of weakness.

"Small return for my exertions this evening, but I can always collect more at my leisure. Can I not, Blue-eyes?"

When she opened her eyes he had gone and she did not have the strength to rise from the bed to watch his departure from the garden below – only to turn her face into the pillows and shed the bitter tears she had never allowed him to witness . . .

CHAPTER
SIX

FOR over a week Babette was subject to constant anguish and misery. Each time Louis returned from Sans Souci she asked after Grant, only to be told that his doctor had confined him to bed and no one had seen him since. He had known how weak he was and what the consequences of his actions would entail, she realised, but he had still visited her to prove he had the upper hand . . . and succeeded. She would never have the courage to act so defiantly again.

When Marguerite began again to visit Sans Souci, Babette knew Grant was improving and had reappeared downstairs among his customers. The misery locked in her heart grew with each passing day as she listened to her sister-in-law's vividly described encounters with her new admirer. She gambled at his tables, dined in his private suite and took moonlit walks with him beside the bayou. Babette feared the day would come when Marguerite would tell her they had become lovers . . .

The sight of a carriage drawing up outside the house one day, almost three weeks after Grant's daring visit to her bedroom, made her grow pale and step back from the window where she had been sitting completing some embroidery. The driver's livery was unmistakable. Panic seized her and by the time she had recovered her composure and hurried downstairs, Jason had already admitted him.

He came into the drawing room, tall and arrogant. His right arm hung stiffly by his side and Babette blanched. At the sight of her his face broke into a smile, but the warmth of it did not reach his eyes.

"Good morning, Mrs. Weldon."

She gave a curt nod, clasping her hands firmly in front of her.

"I suggest you leave immediately, Monsieur Tyler, unless you want me to call the servants and have you thrown out. You are not welcome in this house."

"Your sister-in-law may have another opinion," he mocked.

"Marguerite? You came to see her –" her voice trailed off into a miserable silence. After the other night she had thought –

"Yes, I've come for Marguerite," Grant answered. "I'm not here on your behalf."

"You are disgusting," Babette said bitterly. "Why don't you leave her alone?"

"Because I find her quite – amusing," he answered, his tone growing harsh. "Also, she does not pretend there is any real significance to our relationship, save the ordinary pleasures of life. You would do well to take a leaf from her book; it might improve things between us in the future."

Babette stared at him, aghast. "Relationship," she whispered. "Have you gone that far with her?"

Grant's eyes grew merciless.

"Marguerite has a most appealing way about her," he answered quietly, "and after all, I am only a man."

Babette reeled back, nauseated by his calmness. "She is your mistress," she accused.

A smile crooked Grant's lips. He neither denied nor admitted it.

"Are you jealous, Blue-eyes? Never mind, the more you are, the easier it will be to agree to my terms."

He swung away from her before she could answer, to greet Marguerite who was hurrying downstairs. Babette winced inwardly as he took her in his arms and kissed her. Marguerite freed herself with a soft laugh, but it was obvious that she did not object to his action.

"Grant – not before Babette, she would not understand."

"I think I do," Babette said coldly. "I wonder if Ralph is aware of it."

"Ralph is my brother, not my keeper," Marguerite pouted.

"And Monsieur Tyler is somewhat out of our class. You surprise me, Marguerite. Usually you have better taste."

"Grant is a man who takes what he wants – a real man." Marguerite looked up at him boldly. "I have no complaints. Oh, tell Ralph I may not be back until late. Grant and I are going for a picnic."

"I hope the weather keeps fine for you," Babette said stiffly.

"Do you?" Grant murmured. He tucked Marguerite's arm around his and saw Babette whiten. Her blue eyes searched his face for some sign which would tell her he was only using Marguerite to hurt her – that she meant nothing to him. She saw no such sign and turned away despairingly.

When his day's work was over, Louis had grown accustomed to stopping off at Sans Souci to partake in a glass of wine with his employer. This day being no different to any other, he rode up to the house as dusk was falling, and went straight up to Grant's first-floor apartments. For three consecutive weeks he had drunk in Grant's company, both early in the evening and later when he returned to gamble, but not once had he managed to penetrate the protective shell woven about the other man. Babette was a forbidden subject. Providing no reference was made to her, they were quite amiable in each other's company.

"Good evening, Sam. Monsieur Tyler not here?"

He poured himself a drink and relaxed into a chair before the fire.

Grant's manservant continued to light the candelabra on the dining table.

"He is otherwise occupied for the moment."

"Counting all his money, I'll warrant," Louis laughed. "Lord, I'm hungry, can you rustle up a plate of sandwiches or something?"

Sam hesitated. He wanted to say no and get rid of this man before there was trouble, but the master had said he was always to be made comfortable.

"I'll see what I can find, Mr. St. Clair."

Louis' amused glance followed him out through the door. He was on his fourth drink before Grant appeared, fastening the cuffs of a fresh white silk shirt.

"St. Clair! Why didn't someone tell me you were here? I see you are making yourself at home."

"As usual. Sam said you were otherwise engaged."

"Did he now," Grant frowned; then his face cleared and he was demanding to know how the plantation was progressing. Whenever they broached this subject, Louis found his employer was most at ease. They seemed to share the same desire to make the Sans Souci plantation a paying concern once more.

"I rode past the old house. The workmen have already started on the repairs," Louis said.

Grant nodded.

"It isn't in such a bad state as everyone thinks. I've given them a deadline of six weeks.

"Don't you think that's pushing them rather hard?"

"I have my reasons," the other man answered, but did not enlighten him further. He knew better than to ask.

An hour later Louis rose to take his leave. He found the atmosphere at Sans Souci pleasantly relaxing, but tonight Grant seemed on edge, consuming more whisky than was usual at that time of the evening.

"It's getting late," he said and rose from his chair.

"Grant – how much longer must I stay – ? Oh!"

Louis whirled towards the door as the familiar voice trailed off. Marguerite hesitated for a second, then advanced out of the adjoining bedroom. It was not possible, Louis thought, not Grant and *her*. Cold fury filled his heart. Marguerite lying in his arms, enjoying his lovemaking, while at home his sister moped over a man not fit to kiss her feet.

"I didn't know you had company," Marguerite said softly, slipping down on to the couch beside Grant. She laid her cheek against his shoulder with a sigh. "You were so long, I thought you had forgotten me."

Grant disengaged himself with a tight smile. "Hardly," he returned dryly. If her appearance had annoyed him he did not show it.

"Get her out of here," Louis ordered. "You and I have something to discuss."

He did not expect Grant to obey, but he did.

"Go back and wait for me," Grant said, pulling her to her feet.

"Why can't I stay?" Marguerite protested. She looked suspiciously at Louis. "What have you to say that's so secret?"

"Perhaps you prefer to go home," Grant interrupted and moved towards the bell-rope to summon Sam.

"No – I'll go."

She disappeared into the other room. Grant stared at the closed door, then motioned Louis to follow him and strode out on to the landing.

"Like all women, she is too inquisitive," he said. At the head of the staircase he halted and waited for Louis to join him. "Well, what is it you want to say? I warn you, if it's about Babette, think twice before you speak."

Louis stiffened, his eyes flashing angrily.

"I am demanding satisfaction, Monsieur Tyler."

"Are you really?" Grant did not appear unduly concerned. "Then I believe the choice of weapons is mine."

"Exactly. Swords or pistols, Monsieur?"

"Neither," Grant answered. "If we fight it will be with bare hands and I'll send you back to your precious sister beaten to a pulp. It's time I gave her a reason to hate me."

"Haven't you already? Very well, I accept your offer – bare fists it shall be. At your convenience, Monsieur."

Grant sighed.

"You're a fool, St. Clair, she isn't worth it. You won't win, you know."

"I will take my chances," Louis returned stiffly and turned on his heel.

Grant stared after him, frowning fiercely. He would have preferred to have Louis St. Clair as a friend, rather than an enemy. Over the past weeks his opinion of him had greatly improved. It both angered and saddened him to think he might be forced to beat his foolish brains out in the near future.

"Have you finished your little *tête-à-tête*?" Marguerite came to his side, entwining her arm through his.

"When I tell you to stay out of sight, I mean it," Grant said coldly. "Next time do as you're told."

"What did it matter, it was only Louis. What were you talking about, anyway?"

"Nothing which concerns you."

Marguerite drew back to stare into his face.

"It was another woman. There is someone else, isn't there?"

Yes, Marguerite thought, there was another woman. When he had held her in his arms a short while before he had been preoccupied with other thoughts. She had never known her charms to fail before, yet this man had been withdrawn, his kisses too controlled, satisfying her hunger, but not his own.

"Then I'll make you forget her." She moved against him, pressing her face against his chest. He smelt the sweet fragrance of her hair and slowly his arms closed around her. Marguerite smiled and looked up, her lips parting eagerly. "Forget her, Grant, whoever she is. Am I so ugly in comparison? Shut her out of your life — your thoughts. Let me in."

With something near to a groan, Grant gathered her roughly against him. Perhaps it wouldn't be possible to obliterate Babette completely from his mind, but he could try.

The moment Babette heard Louis' horse turn into the cob-
blestone courtyard she flew out on to the porch.

"Louis – oh, Louis! Come quickly!"

"What is it, *ma petite*? Why, you're trembling."

She plucked at his coat with nerveless fingers, her eyes
wide and frightened.

"It's Ralph and father, they are in the study quarrelling.
The door is locked and they won't let me in. If father gets too
excited – Oh, Louis, his heart!"

Her brother wasted no time asking questions. He strode to
the study and hammered fiercely on the door.

"Ralph, open up or I'll break it down!"

The angry voices on the other side of the panels abruptly
died away. Babette clutched his arm apprehensively.

"Make him leave father alone."

"He's asking to have his scrawny neck wrung," Louis
muttered. "*Mon dieu*! Haven't I enough to cope with!"

Babette was too overwrought to apply any special significance to his words. She only knew her father's heart
was weak and liable to stop his life short without warning.
Ralph knew how delicate he was, yet here they were
arguing.

"Are you coming out – ?" Louis began, but he never
completed the sentence. The study door opened and Ralph
emerged, swaying drunkenly. Babette reeled back from the
odour of whisky about him.

"Your father has need of you," he sneered, and staggered
past them towards the front door. Louis turned after him in a
blind fury, his fists clenched to strike him.

"Louis!" Babette's agonised cry sent him rushing into the
study. She was kneeling on the floor over their father's inert
form. The room screamed chaos. Books fallen from their
shelves, chairs overturned, ornaments smashed.

"He's blind drunk – mad –" Louis said, horrified.

"Never mind, help me with father. He doesn't answer me.
Oh, Louis – he's dead!"

Her brother bent beside her, reaching for his father's

wrist. A slow beat of life flickered uncertainly beneath his fingers.

"He's alive! Send Jemima for the doctor and tell a couple of boys to come and help me get him upstairs. Hurry now, there's a good girl. Don't worry, he's a tough old man."

Babette threw him a grateful look before she ran to do his bidding. His calmness had quietened her momentary hysteria. But later, while she waited anxiously in the drawing room for the doctor's report, her self-control began to snap.

Louis saw huge tears begin to roll down her cheeks and rose from his chair.

"Hold on, *mignonne*, it won't be long now."

"He's been in there for over an hour." Babette hid her face against his chest. "I'm afraid, Louis. I think he's going to die. I can feel it."

"Nonsense. He's had these turns before and got over them."

"Not this time. Ralph has killed him, and all for nothing."

Louis took her firmly by the arm and sat her down in a chair.

"Don't you think you'd better tell me what you mean?"

"They were quarrelling over ownership of the Line," she said, in a more controlled tone. "They were talking so loudly it was easy to hear every word. Ralph is short of money. He wanted father to relinquish the partnership and make him sole owner."

"And our father refused, of course."

"He had to. He doesn't own it any more, Louis. Grant Tyler bought him out over a month ago."

Louis stared at her incredulously.

"Tyler! What does he want with half ownership in a shipping line?"

"He means to force Ralph out and take it over himself."

Louis poured himself a large drink and gulped it back, cursing Grant Tyler's name. He meant trouble and it was directed at his sister. He turned slowly and looked at her.

"Is there something you haven't told me?"

She paled considerably. "What do you need to know? He's out to hurt me because I married Ralph. It's as simple as that."

"Why does he bother when he's already found other amusement?" Louis replied and could have bitten off his tongue for such thoughtless words.

"It's all right, I know. He came for Marguerite this afternoon. He didn't even try to hide the fact she's his mistress."

"Babette, I'm sorry – he's the spawn of the devil. I could kill him, and that she-cat of a sister-in-law. When I saw them together –"

Babette looked up questioningly.

"You saw them? Where?"

"At Sans Souci. You know I stop by in the evenings before coming home. From the moment Grant came into the room I had the impression I wasn't welcome; then when Marguerite appeared I knew why."

Babette closed her eyes, fighting back a rush of tears. Together at Sans Souci, not at a picnic as Marguerite had said. The last shadow of doubt as to their relationship vanished from her mind.

She was not allowed to indulge in self-pity, however, for the doctor appeared. Etienne St. Clair had suffered a severe stroke which had left him totally paralysed and with less than a fighting chance of recovery.

"He is going to die, then," Louis said, his lips tightening.

"It is more than likely," came the grave reply. "I shall be back in the morning. Until then someone must stay at his side constantly."

Babette volunteered, and refused to be swayed from her decision. Throughout the long night she sat at her father's bedside, holding one of his cold hands in hers, praying that somewhere someone would be merciful. With trembling fingers she touched the lank grey hair and traced the outline of the face which was so dear to her. As surely as she had once ruined Louis' happiness, so she had now brought her father to his present unhappy state.

During the past year they had drifted apart, and she bitterly reproached herself for allowing it to happen. Instead of giving him the love and understanding he so badly needed, she had selfishly put herself and her own demands first, blaming him when she grew discontented and miserable. Now, perhaps, it was too late to make amends. He would never know how deeply she still loved him, and the knowledge he had died without realising it would haunt her forever.

Towards morning she drifted into a light sleep but awakened as the bedroom door opened behind her. Louis tiptoed to the bedside. In the grey light of dawn she saw his face was drawn and haggard.

"How is he, Babette?"

"Still sleeping. He doesn't even know I'm here." She fought to control the tremor in her voice. "Why don't you try to rest, *mon frère*."

"I was about to suggest the same to you," Louis answered with a faint smile. "Jemima can sit with him until the doctor comes. In fact I insist, you look worn out."

"Very well, but only if you're sure he will be all right."

Louis slipped an arm around her shoulders and led her out into the passageway. "He's in God's hands. They are good hands."

"Where is Ralph?"

"Out – Marguerite too."

I know where she is, Babette thought and shivered. It was still too horrible to believe.

"Will you try and rest, too?" she asked.

Louis nodded, pushing her gently towards her room. "In a while, I promise. Go to bed now."

He waited until she had entered her room before going into the study. A glass of whisky gave him the necessary courage to write the note to Grant Tyler arranging the time and place for the settlement of their differences. He wanted it over and done with quickly.

Purely by chance, Babette encountered Jason who had

been entrusted to deliver the important message. She had
gone into Louis' room to reassure herself he was also resting,
but found he was not there. Intent on finding him, she turned
to go downstairs and almost collided with Jason, hurrying
towards the back staircase.

"Jason – is anything wrong? My father isn't worse?"

"Lordy no, Miss B'bette. I'm on my way out for Mr.
Louis."

"At this time of morning! Is it to fetch the doctor?"
Babette could not understand her brother dispensing with
the needed presence of the servants.

Jason held up the note he was to deliver.

"Mr. Louis says I'm to give this to a certain gentleman at
Sans Souci and bring back an answer."

Babette had no doubt as to the identity of the certain
gentleman. Plucking the note from Jason's fingers, she slit
open the envelope and read the contents of the letter. Louis'
arranging to settle with Grant Tyler at six a.m. – the words
chilled her. It could only mean one thing – a duel. But why?
When had they quarrelled? He had told her of no arguments.

"Where is my brother now?" she asked.

"In the study. He's –" Jason thought of Louis downstairs,
intent on emptying the decanter of whisky. "He seemed to be
resting. Leave him be, Miss B'bette, you've both had a tiring
night."

"I have no intention of disturbing him, Jason. Wait for me
in the kitchen, I'll join you in a few minutes."

"But the letter –" Jason protested too late – the door of
Babette's room closed behind her.

Ten minutes later she came down to the kitchen fully
dressed and wearing a fur-lined cloak.

"You will escort me to Sans Souci," she said quietly, and
proceeded out of the back door.

Muttering to himself, Jason followed her at a distance. He
had seen a familiar gleam in her eyes and knew from past
experience that further argument would be a waste of time
and breath.

Babette hurried ahead of him without a backward glance. It would be light in a few hours. Before then she had to talk to Grant – persuade him to abandon the idea of a duel. She had no idea what course of action to take. If he refused a straight-forward request, she would be lost.

At the beginning of the driveway she stopped and turned to Jason.

"Give me my brother's letter."

"But Mr. Louis said –"

"Jason, don't be difficult. Go back and give Louis this message. Mr. Tyler regrets the misunderstanding which has arisen between them and apologises – therefore there is no need to keep the appointment. Do you understand?"

Jason repeated it slowly. "What about you, Miss B'bette? I can't leave you here alone."

"As far as you're concerned, you haven't seen me," Babette answered firmly. "My brother must believe I am asleep in my room."

At least part of her plan had succeeded, Babette thought, hurrying on towards the house. Louis' non-appearance might avert the duel altogether, if only she could be sure of Grant's co-operation.

A carriage was drawn up outside the front entrance. Cautiously she hid behind the bushes, waiting for it to depart. On no account did she want to be seen entering a gaming house, alone and unprotected, at four o'clock in the morning.

The murmur of voices arrested her attention. Three figures came out into the open. In the light from the huge lantern swinging over the door they were immediately recognisable. Ralph, leaning heavily on Grant's shoulder and Marguerite.

"My coachman will take you home," Babette heard Grant say.

"Bless you." Marguerite leant up on tiptoe to kiss him. "I don't want to leave, but I suppose someone has to take him home. I still don't understand what he was babbling about – do you?"

"It was the drink talking. He'll be fine in the morning," Grant returned and closed the carriage door behind them.

There was another exchange of words, too low for Babette to catch. Marguerite leant out of the window and Babette watched Grant move forward to kiss her again. Then without waiting to watch the carriage depart, he strode back into the house.

Drawing her cloak tighter around her, Babette came out of hiding and moved towards the door. It was still open. A few feet away Grant stood smoking and silently surveying the deserted gaming tables. His back was towards her.

She moistened her lips, dreading the moments ahead.

"Monsieur Tyler!"

How formal and unreal his name sounded.

Grant wheeled about with a low oath as her voice shattered his intense thoughts.

"You!" he said unbelievingly. "What do you want?"

"I must talk with you." She held out the letter. "I've brought this."

He took it and read it through several times in silence, before asking coldly,

"Did Louis send you here?"

"Of course not, he thinks I'm in bed alseep."

"Where all good little girls should be," Grant remarked cynically. "Go upstairs. We can't talk here. I'll follow when I've given Sam instructions to close up. You know the way, of course," he added when she did not move.

He expected a sharp retort and was surprised when none came. Without a word she crossed the hall and went up the marble staircase to his apartments. When Grant entered the drawing room Babette was seated on the couch before the fire, hugging her cloak about her as if hoping it would make her invisible.

Wordlessly he crossed to the decanter and poured a large amount of brandy into a glass.

"Thank you, no," Babette said when he held it out to her.

"I take it you didn't come here to argue," he retorted and

thrust it into her hand. Then he poured himself a drink and sat opposite her.

"How did you come to be in possession of Louis' letter?"

"I intercepted it. What does it mean?" Her eyes searched his bleak face. "Do you intend to fight him?"

"Your brother must take full credit for the suggestion. He took offence at something I said."

"Concerning me?" Babette broke in. "You goaded him into it!"

"I repeat, your brother must take full credit," Grant snapped. "I have no wish to hurt him – you are my target."

Babette winced at his words and swallowed down the brandy so quickly it stung her throat and brought a rush of tears to her eyes.

"He will not be coming," she said at length.

Grant surveyed her from beneath arched brows.

"Tell me more. How have you persuaded him to hide?"

"He isn't hiding. I sent back an answer, pretending it came from you." Her voice dropped to a mere whisper. "I apologised in your place."

"The devil you did!" Grant answered coldly. "I do my own apologising when I deem it necessary – which I don't in this case. It will take more than your intervention to stop me this time."

Slowly Babette rose, dropped her cloak on to the couch and went to pour herself another brandy. She seldom touched spirits, but tonight she needed more courage than ever before in her young life.

She swayed back to her seat and sat down while Grant watched her with a puzzled frown. What did she hope to gain by coming to him? Once Louis learnt of the deception he would not hesitate to demand satisfaction again. Perhaps she had come armed with her Derringer to make another attempt on his life, he mused humourlessly. When she looked at him, however, he saw utter despair in her eyes.

"Have you come to beg?" he asked cruelly.

"If I have to," Babette answered. "I want you to leave

Louis, all my family, alone. As you've just said – I am your target. Take your hate out on me – not them. Please." Her voice broke and Grant saw tears in her eyes before she lowered her head. The sight of them did not soften his heart. They were a woman's weapon when all other resources failed. Even Marguerite had resorted to them several times in the short space of their relationship.

He leaned back in his chair and lighted a cheroot, watching her through half-closed eyes. She seemed to grow thinner each time he saw her. Perhaps she was ill – or pregnant? No – she was too thin for that. His blood boiled to think she might carry any child other than his own.

"Does that request include your husband?" he asked.

"I am too tired to argue with you, Monsieur Tyler, I ask only that, if you must hurt someone, let it be me. Not those close to me." Babette thought of her father as she spoke. Would they ever be close again?

"It has to be unconditional surrender, Blue-eyes."

She nodded mutely. She no longer had a choice.

"Whatever you say."

Grant was silent for a long while. Somehow this moment of triumph was not as soul raising as he had expected.

"You must love him very much."

"I do. Louis and I have always been close – even as children. Does this mean you won't fight him?"

"It does – and I wasn't referring to your brother." He flung her a puzzled, angry glance. Was she being deliberately misleading?

"What do you want me to do now?" she asked, staring fixedly at the fire.

"I suggest you go home and get some rest, you look exhausted. I'll have my housekeeper fix you a hot toddy. When my coachman returns I am sending you straight home."

Babette could not believe her ears. "You don't want me to stay?"

Grant gave her a crooked smile and rose to his feet. "A

good gambler never overplays his hand," he answered in a mocking tone. "I know where to find you. Stay here, I'll only be a moment."

Her mind reeling, Babette watched the door close behind him. Why did he hesitate now she was his? Was it to deliberately unnerve her? If so, it had succeeded. Wearily her head drooped down on to the arm of the couch. It was over and Louis was to be spared the ordeal of a duel. There was no reason for him to know she had ever visited Sans Souci and she could pretend her differences with Grant had been resolved.

Grant returned to find her sound asleep. For a moment he stood at her side, an odd smile playing round the corners of his mouth, before covering her with her cloak and returning to the chair by the fire.

The hot drink Sam brought he drank himself and gave orders not to bother sending the coachman to him when he returned. He sat before the crackling flames, with the curtains drawn back from the windows, watching the gradual lightening of the sky. This was the last time, he told himself. His mind could rest at ease now. His gaze strayed continually to Babette's sleeping form. Something was troubling her, and it was not to do with him.

He was dozing when Sam announced Louis' arrival. With a sigh Grant straightened to meet the onslaught he felt sure must be forthcoming. A quick look at his watch told him it had been three hours since Babette arrived at Sans Souci.

"Have you come to work or fight?" he drawled when his visitor strode through the door.

"Where is she?" Louis was in no mood for argument. His gaze fell on the sleeping Babette. "In heaven's name, what have you done to her?"

"She's sleeping, and has been for several hours."

Louis shouldered past him, ignoring the cold glint which flashed into Grant's eyes as he was pushed aside. Kneeling beside the couch, he gently shook Babette into wakefulness.

"Louis!" She started up in alarm. "What are you doing

here? You don't have to fight. Grant – Monsieur Tyler has apologised."

"Hush, child. I've no stomach for a fight just now."

Something in his tone halted Babette's flow of words. Apprehensively she caught his hand. Louis glanced up at Grant who had moved beside them.

"She's going to need a drink," he said quietly.

Babette knew, even before he broke the dreadful news to her.

"*Ma petite*, you must be brave. I've come to take you home. Our father is dead."

CHAPTER
SEVEN

THE funeral of Etienne St. Clair took place a week later, attended only by members of his family. Babette had scarcely spoken a word to anyone since Louis had taken her from Sans Souci. Grant's softly spoken words of sympathy scarcely registered on her stunned mind as he wrapped her cloak close round her shivering body and helped her downstairs to the waiting carriage. She did not cry – not then, nor during the days which followed. Long days, spent in the solitude of her room, alone with her grief. She gained comfort from nobody – not even from Louis. Her father was dead and she had failed to be with him. Perhaps he had wanted her, she would never know.

On the morning of the funeral she arose from her bed, drawn and tired. Jemima helped her to dress without her usual careless chatter, her coal-black features lined with worry.

Throughout the short service and afterwards, standing beside the enormous vaults which sometimes rose in tiers as high as twelve feet from the ground – for, due to the wetness of the surrounding terrain, the dead in New Orleans did not find their final resting place in the earth – Babette felt as if she was in another world, a frightening world of shadows where nothing was real. She was not aware of people around her, of quietly whispered words of sympathy, not even of the touch of Louis' hand on hers . . . Not until they had returned to the house did some vestige of feeling return slowly to her limbs.

"Babette – bear with us a while longer." Louis was beside her, a comforting arm around her waist. "There is the reading of the will yet. The others are waiting for us in the study. Afterwards it will be over."

No, you're wrong, Babette thought silently. It will be the beginning. Grant will see to that. But the beginning of what?

At the door of the study Louis laid a detaining hand on her arm.

"Before you go in, I must tell you – Monsieur Tyler is here."

"But why, surely the will does not involve him?"

"Apparently it does. Will you be all right?"

Babette nodded and preceded him into the room. Grant pulled out a chair for her. She hesitated and then sat down, acknowledging his action with a slight nod.

Vincent Abelard, the family lawyer, regarded them over the rims of large horn-rimmed glasses.

"Are we all here? Mr. and Mrs. Weldon – Miss Weldon, Mr. St. Clair and Mr. Tyler. Yes – all here."

Ralph, seated on the low, curving window seat beside his sister, glared across at Grant.

"Why is his presence necessary? He isn't family."

"Why not wait and find out?" Louis retorted.

Marguerite caught her brother's arm with a reproving look.

"Not now, Ralph – later. Have you forgotten you are now the sole owner of the St. Clair Shipping Line? Our impetuous brother-in-law obviously has. He'll soon come to heel when he realises you control all business interests and all money."

Ralph settled back in his seat, chuckling softly. "Sometimes you surprise me, sister dear."

"Just make sure I'm not left short of anything I need," she murmured meaningly.

The lawyer cleared his throat, thrust his spectacles more firmly on to the bridge of his nose and unfolded several pieces of paper on the desk before him.

Babette turned enquiringly to Louis. "I don't understand. Father told us that when – when he died, we would share everything. Why is there need for a will?"

Louis met Grant's expressionless gaze over her shoulders. He shook his head.

"Apart from a few small bequests to servants, the residue of the late Mr. St. Clair's estate goes to his daughter, Mrs. Weldon."

Five pairs of eyes fixed themselves on the lawyer.

"I don't understand." It was Babette who broke the silence. "To me?"

"It's a mistake!" Ralph leapt to his feet and snatched up the will.

"As you can see for yourself, the terms are as I've stated." Vincent Abelard said coldly.

"What's this about a letter?" Ralph demanded. He had grown extremely pale and was trembling with anger. Standing by the window, Grant surveyed them all emotionlessly.

The lawyer produced a sealed envelope which he held well out of reach of Ralph's grasp.

"Mr. St. Clair left this for his daughter. He states on the envelope that he'd like to have it read aloud – as it concerns everyone in this room."

Louis crossed to the table, examined the envelope and looked enquiringly at his sister.

Babette shook her head.

"Please read it, Monsieur Abelard."

Across the room she met Grant's eyes. They held sympathy for her, as they had done the night Louis came to find her. She hated him for pretending he was concerned. No doubt he was inwardly enjoying her distressed condition and wondering how he could pile further miseries on her head.

"Shall I begin, Mrs. Weldon?" the lawyer asked gently.

"Yes – please."

" 'My dear Babette,

'I am writing this, my last letter to you instead of to Louis, for I know he will understand how important it is for me to make my peace with you. Forgiveness will not come easily from you – I understand this and I do not expect it. I only hope and pray that, in time, you will be able to remember me without too much bitterness in your heart.

'Over the past year we have grown apart. This, I feel, is my fault. You are young and impulsive. I was wrong, terribly wrong, to hold you responsible for what happened. It is even worse that you are paying the price for the happiness of someone dear to us both. Whatever you may believe, I love both my children deeply. It is a comfort to me that you will have Louis to care for you and see you do not suffer further!' ''

"Is Monsieur Tyler there?" The lawyer raised his head with a faint smile. "This is still part of the letter, you understand?"

Grant nodded and lighted a fresh cheroot. He could not tear his eyes away from Babette's distraught features.

" 'Monsieur Tyler is there with you because, as he has probably told you by now, I sold him my half of the business. Forgive me, my dear, but the need for money was too great. I need hardly tell you where it all went. I, too, am paying a heavy price. Later, when I needed more, I found it necessary to mortgage everything. Once again Monsieur Tyler came to my aid. I had hoped to repay him, but now I know it is too late. He is a fair man – I am sure he will not take advantage of your present unfortunate position –' ''

"I've heard enough!" Ralph shouted roughly. "The old man was mad – out of his head."

"My father was of sound mind right up to the last," Babette answered coldly.

Ralph wheeled on her.

"And how would you know? You weren't even with him."

"I think you've said quite enough." Louis rose to his feet, prepared for a fight. "Is that the full text of the letter, Monsieur Abelard?"

"The rest is of a sentimental nature which I'm sure Mrs. Weldon will prefer to read alone – at a later date."

Babette reached for the letter with a shaking hand, forcing herself to ask, "Just how much has my father left?"

"Exactly eight hundred and thirty-five dollars – plus your mother's jewellery, which I believe is already in your possession."

"This is incredible," Ralph blurted out. "Where has it all gone?"

"Don't you know?" Babette's tone was accusing. Her father's letter had explained matters only too clearly. They were all no better than paupers – even the house belonged to Grant Tyler. He had set out to ruin her family and succeeded with incredible simplicity. "Who paid your gambling debts, Ralph, whose money set up a girl called Rachel in a quiet little house on the other side of town?" By the sudden pallor which crept into Ralph's cheeks, she knew her guess about the house was correct. "Oh, don't bother to deny it, I've seen you together. Not that it matters. Nothing matters any more."

For the first time in seven long days, Louis saw tears in her eyes. Gently he drew her head against his shoulder.

"If there is nothing else, Monsieur Abelard, perhaps you would be good enough to leave us, my sister is naturally upset. The housekeeper will show you out."

"I, too, must take my leave." Grant extinguished his half-smoked cheroot and moved towards the door.

"Just a moment." Ralph stepped in front of him. "I want a word with you."

Grant's eyes narrowed sharply at his offensive tone. He wanted nothing better than an excuse for a fight with this man.

"Do you think you can afford my time?" he asked.

"Why, you insolent – ! I don't take that talk from your kind." A heavy hand was laid on Grant's shoulder. With deliberate slowness he removed it and dusted down his coat.

"Don't do that again, little man," he drawled insolently.

Ralph flushed. It was not often any man went against him so openly. He wanted to lash out at Marguerite's smiling face. Her time would come, along with the rest, but first he had to gain absolute control of the shipping line. He needed the money desperately, for his own needs and Rachel's. Daily she became more demanding – not that he minded, for she carried out her part of the bargain in a fashion that was immensely satisfying. His prudish wife rarely occupied his thoughts nowadays. He gave a slight bow and even managed to smile.

"My apologies, Monsieur – this has been a trying time for me," he said suavely. "Will you not stay and take a glass of sherry with us? I have something I wish to talk over with you."

"Father has been in his grave only a few hours, can't it wait?" Babette broke in horrified.

Ralph scarcely looked at her. "You are overwrought, my dear. I suggest you go to your room."

Hardly the attentive husband, Grant thought ironically and wondered if she had ever regretted the band of gold on her finger which bound her to this selfish, vain excuse for a man. Perhaps as a lover he made up for the qualities sadly lacking as a husband. The thought was not a pleasant one.

"Whatever you intend to say, Babette and I will both hear it," Louis said, stepping forward. The first shock of the surprise will had diminished. Their father had been a shrewd business man and he had not entrusted his half of the company to this gambler just for the money. With luck, Ralph's dream of becoming sole owner might never materialise.

Grant took out his watch and studied it. "I have an appointment in an hour," he said shortly.

Time enough for Ralph to buy you out, Louis thought, and discovered he was hoping it would not happen. Aloud he said, "Why don't we adjourn to the drawing room?"

Marguerite took Grant's arm, hurrying him ahead of the others.

"Are you anxious to learn the price of my half of the business?" he asked dryly.

"Nonsense, of course not. This is the first time I've seen you in five whole days."

"Sans Souci hasn't moved."

"I know." She grew irritated at his casual manner. "Ralph gave me a lecture on propriety, but it didn't stop him going to his fancy woman last night. Can we meet later?"

"Your eagerness to be with me is touching," Grant murmured. "I seem to recall you broke our last date."

"I've told you, Ralph is being difficult." The lie came easily to Marguerite's lips. To share in his newly acquired wealth she would sell her soul to the devil. "Please, Grant, I have a new gown."

"Doubtless I am paying for it."

"Not unless you think it's worth it."

"Wear it tonight and I'll tell you." Grant caught the glimpse of satisfaction which flashed into her eyes and inwardly chuckled. He was too old to be caught by such an amateur trick, but it amused him to play along – until evening came, and then, he decided, it would be time for a showdown.

Watching them together, Babette felt sick with disgust. Louis fetched her a drink and stood beside her chair.

"It might have proved simpler in the long run to let us fight," he said quietly. He, too, was annoyed by Grant's open attentions to his sister-in-law. In Sans Souci it was different, but to act in this way before the girl who had once loved him was unforgivable. It seemed all his actions were deliberately insulting; meant to cause her pain. Louis was puzzled – such a love was not the kind he had experienced. His memories were treasured, not used to inspire hate or revenge. God knows he had every right to feel that way.

Impatiently he turned on Ralph.

"Get on with it," he said ungraciously and swung round on Grant. "There seems to be some difficulty in broaching the subject," he went on. "Ever since father was forced to take on a partner, Ralph has seen himself as the head of the St. Clair Shipping Line – a wealthy and all-powerful figure in New Orleans." His lip curled scornfully. "Father rudely shattered his dream, Monsieur Tyler. Of course he could sell his half to you, but somehow I think he prefers it to be the other way round."

Grant savoured his sherry for a moment, aware of the

tension in the atmosphere. The look Ralph threw Louis left everyone in no doubt as to his thoughts.

"A somewhat blunt assessment of what I wanted to say." Ralph turned apologetically to his newly acquired partner. "Name your price, Monsieur."

"I doubt if you could meet it," Grant returned. "Besides, Etienne St. Clair asked me when he sold out, not to let you have it at any price. I respect his wishes. I'm sorry, Weldon, but no deal. Of course, if you should decide to sell your half I'll buy you out."

Ralph's lips tightened. This man was making him look a fool and everyone in the room knew it. "I'll top whatever you paid," he said hoarsely.

Grant stubbornly shook his head. "I'm not interested in money, I have enough. If I do relinquish my interests, it won't be for hard cash." For an instant his eyes held Babette's. For you I would give it up, came the silent message, only for you.

"It's not only a question of the business," Louis said. "You own our house – the land. Why did you buy them?"

"To help your father out of a hole. He needed cash in a hurry and I provided it. I fully expected him to repay me before long."

"Are we to leave, then?" Babette broke her silence for the first time.

"I have a house – two, in fact. This one is of no use to me. No one need ever know there has been any financial difficulty beneath this roof. Should you one day find the money to repay me, then the property will once more revert to the family. I hope you manage to do so."

"Do you?" Babette was not convinced.

A tiny frown puckered Grant's brows at the rising note of hysteria in her voice. "I am not an unreasonable man," he said quietly.

"For a gambler you appear to have a head for business," Ralph broke in.

Grant gave a slight bow. "I never overlook an opportunity," he answered. "Now, if you will excuse me, I really must leave."

"Of course – we would not dream of keeping you from an appointment," Babette said icily. "Allow me to see you to the door."

She stood by patiently while he took his leave of the others, her lips tightening as he deliberately lingered with Marguerite.

"Perhaps you will enlighten me on one point." Grant paused by the front door and looked at Babette. "Why was it necessary for your father to apologise to you?"

A faint flush of colour stole into Babette's ashen cheeks.

"It is a personal matter – extremely personal."

"I was thinking he had chastised you for some indiscreet incident in your impetuous past and perhaps regretted it ever since. Tell me, have you ever been a naughty girl? Is that why Weldon married you – to make you a respectable lady of the town?"

His sarcasm passed over Babette's head. She was too weary and grief stricken to retaliate.

"Whatever the reason, Monsieur Tyler, it does not concern you. We had something once, but it ceased to exist long ago."

"We had nothing," Grant returned harshly. "You amused me – nothing more. Amusement is all I expect from a woman, none of you are capable of any real feelings."

Babette flung wide the door and stood back for him to pass. "Please leave and don't come back."

"One thing you cannot do, is to forbid me my own house," Grant answered quietly, and with that parting shot he walked out.

Marguerite was in high spirits when Sam showed her into the drawing room at Sans Souci, but all her hopes for a resounding victory over Grant were quickly squashed by his sombre mood. Throughout dinner he was unusually quiet, and Marguerite began to grow restless.

"My dress must be more stunning than I thought," she

said when he lingered over his coffee instead of joining her on the couch.

"I have something on my mind," he returned, but after a while he sat down beside her. Marguerite moved closer, pressing her body against his, and he did not refuse the invitation.

She did not know as he kissed her, that he was remembering another night – the last night of Mardi Gras when Babette had sat in the same spot and told him they must part for ever. The thought of it made him draw back from the willing girl in his arms. Babette had betrayed him with another man. In retaliation, he had used Marguerite to try and forget a heartache which he had learnt could not be forgotten.

"I've something for you," Grant produced a small jewel box from an inside pocket and held it out towards her, "to celebrate my new position."

"Oh, Grant! You are sweet – a diamond clasp." She flung her arms about his neck, overcome with delight. This was the most expensive item so far. Gently but firmly, he disengaged himself.

"Let me fasten it on your dress."

Marguerite's eyes flashed triumphantly as she stared down at the clasp. She would find no better time to approach him. "Sometimes I almost think you like me," she murmured.

Grant smiled and replenished their empty glasses. "Any man who isn't attracted to you is a fool."

"And you don't mind being seen in the company of a poor girl?"

He regarded her with arched brows. "Poor? No poor girl wears a diamond clip."

"I couldn't possibly part with anything you have given me, but of course I will have to sell most of my other jewellery."

Grant thought of Babette who had also tried to sell her valuable possessions, only in her case it had been a genuine attempt to help her brother out of trouble and she had done so without telling anyone. How like Marguerite to play for sympathy, he mused.

"If you are in need of money –" he began.

"Not money – security." Marguerite looked up at him, suddenly serious. "Do you fully understand what the old man's will means? Ralph has no money, only his half of the Line. How long will it be before he mortgages that for gambling money? When he does, I shall be a pauper. I have no money of my own and he gives me very little, just enough for clothes."

A tiny smile twitched at the corners of Grant's mouth. "Then you will be forced to sell even my trinkets," he said, in a low amused tone.

"You can't mean that!" Marguerite was taken aback. She knew he was no fool, but this was not the reaction she had expected. "You wouldn't care?"

"Did you expect me to?" He lighted a cheroot and wandered across to the fire. "I pay for your company the same as any other man, we agreed from the start that's how it would be between us. What you do with your ill-gotten gains afterwards is entirely your affair."

"You can't treat me the same as all your other women," Marguerite retorted, springing to her feet.

"You are no different. You have a better background, breeding and an influential name, but none of these count when one makes love. You're a woman who must have a man – any man."

"I want you," Marguerite said, and moved closer. If she could make him believe that, there was a chance. "I can't deny my mistakes, but I can stop myself from making more in the future – with your help."

"You're about to make a big one now," Grant answered. "Be a sensible girl, Maggie, and call it quits with a good grace."

"Don't call me that," Marguerite began. Then she broke off, the colour receding from her face. "Quits!" she echoed. "What do you mean? You can't throw me over."

"I'm not. I'm simply telling you, we're through. That diamond clip should take care of any hurt feelings."

"Why you – !" Marguerite drew back her hand to strike

him. With a laugh he avoided the blow, grabbed her around the waist and kissed her into silence.

"Believe me, you will never go hungry," he said, releasing her. "There will be others after me."

"Are you going back – to her?" Marguerite sneered. She was no longer pretty when she was angry. Heavy creases furrowed her forehead and her mouth became a thin, taut line. She was not used to being discarded like a worn-out glove.

"If I was, I wouldn't tell you. We've had fun, Maggie, let's leave it at that and say goodnight and goodbye."

"You really mean it! Do you think I'll let you do this to me?"

Grant smiled and moved towards her. "Don't threaten me, or I might take back my clip," he said.

"You wouldn't dare!" Marguerite cried, but her fears were unfounded. He merely picked up her cloak and placed it around her shoulders.

"I arranged to have your carriage here by eleven o'clock."

"How convenient," Marguerite said scathingly. She was trembling with anger. How dare he treat her like a common tramp. "I suppose you've made other arrangements for the rest of the evening."

"I have." Grant ushered her out of the room, a hand solicitously beneath her elbow. She shrugged it off and stalked to the head of the stairs. Not only had she failed to persuade him to sell his half of the Line, he had not even allowed her to broach the subject. Instead she had been given an expensive piece of jewellery and told to run away and play in someone else's back yard.

"You won't forget me. I'll still come to Sans Souci," she threatened.

"Please do. I shall be glad to see you at the gaming tables," Grant answered coolly. He was not in the least perturbed by her anger and after she had gone, all thought of her vanished from his mind. She might never have existed.

CHAPTER
EIGHT

JUST before dawn, Grant left Sans Souci and strode quickly down the driveway towards the centre of the town. Apart from the people still at his gaming tables, there were few others about and he encountered no one he knew. He passed the Weldon house without giving it more than a cursory glance and cut down a side street into the Avenue Briand. This was the end of the select district – beyond lay the poor part of the town with its numerous coloured inhabitants, weaned in the knowledge of voodoo – infamous streets with their even more infamous women, who were not so blackly painted that they were altogether shunned by the men of society.

Grant let himself into Rachel's house by the back door and stood for a moment, listening to the murmur of voices from one of the upstairs rooms. Standing in the shadows by the kitchen door, he watched Rachel and Ralph come down-stairs, heard her soft laughter as Ralph seized her for a last embrace, then the front door closed behind him and she turned into the drawing room rearranging her negligée around her.

She gave a start as Grant appeared behind her. "How long have you been here?"

"A couple of minutes. I witnessed the last touching scene."

"You cut it fine. What if he'd seen you, it would have ruined everything," Rachel began indignantly, but her pro-tests died at the laughter in Grant's face. "How did I sound?"

"Very convincing," Grant said and sank down into a chair. Rachel poured him a drink and one for herself.

"This is like old times." She sat opposite him, conscious of his raised eyebrows as the silk negligée fell away from slim, shapely legs. "I can remember a time you didn't mind."

"Six years is a long time – a lot can happen."

"To Grant Tyler! How true. Since I saw you, you've become quite a gentleman. Sans Souci is an established gaming house, catering for even the most select townsfolk, not like San Francisco where it was a back room and a poker game." Rachel tossed back her drink and put the glass to one side, her green eyes narrowing. "You've come up in the world, lover. A gambling house, plantations, a new palatial residence nearing completion, everything a man could want. Do I know her?"

"I doubt it." Grant did not bother to deny there was a woman any longer.

She looked at him, openly puzzled. "Has success gone to your head, or is she putting up a fight? I've never known you resort to these methods before. Where does Ralph come into it? I mean, what do you get out of collecting his bills, besides ruining him?"

"Satisfaction," he returned. "Have you got them?"

She nodded and rose to take a sheaf of papers from the bureau. Grant thumbed through them and his face broke into a smile. The situation was improving.

"Will you need any more? He's started complaining," Rachel said.

"I doubt it. Adding these to the gambling I.O.U.s I hold, he's heading for a fall."

"What will you get out of it – his wife?"

"What did you say?" Grant gained his feet with startling rapidity and Rachel cried out as his fingers fastened painfully on her arm.

"Ouch – you hurt! Still the same masterful nature, I see."

"Answer me!"

"For heaven's sake, isn't it obvious? A woman's instinct reacts to this kind of situation. I'm paid, and handsomely too, to amuse a comparatively wealthy, utterly boring man who has two loves – money and women. I start to ask myself why. Grant Tyler, a man I know from the old days, a fair hand with the cards, a ruthless business man and a man who has more than his share of women – why should he want to ruin Ralph Weldon? For money gain?" she shrugged. "I doubt it. Besides, this man owes him a considerable sum in gambling debts. Because he doesn't like him? I cast that aside too. The Grant I knew would simply whip him with his fists and forget about him. I don't think you've changed so greatly."

Grant's lips twitched. Releasing her he lighted a fresh cheroot. Rachel resumed her seat, rubbing her bruised wrist.

"You've developed a fresh talent, my dear. Go on – why else should I want to ruin him?"

"He has a wife?" Rachel said quietly. She vaguely remembered seeing Ralph accompanied by a pretty dark-haired girl on one occasion. "French, isn't she? He doesn't talk about her – as far as I recall he's never once mentioned her name."

"He's probably frightened you'd be jealous."

"What, me – of her? She looked a pathetic little thing. She's very young, isn't she? Younger than any other woman you've known."

"You've made up your mind I know her." Grant neither admitted nor denied it. It still hurt to think of Babette, let alone say her name aloud. He had used Marguerite to try and forget her and it had proved an unsuccessful venture, expensive and often irritating.

"I think you are in love – perhaps for the first time in your life." Rachel gave a soft laugh and leant towards him. "Come now, admit it. This French girl has you beaten." She was surprised and shocked at the bitter expression which crossed Grant's features.

"No woman will ever do that to me," he answered in a harsh tone, and she knew it was not love which spurred him on to desperate measures, but revenge. She laid a hand on his arm, her long painted nails caressing the dark hairs on his skin. Often during their association during the past years she had thought it would be nice to have him as a lover, but he had always remained beyond her reach. When she needed help, financial or otherwise, he had always supplied it without the question of repayment ever arising. Perhaps she was settling part of her great debt to him now, but in doing so she was destroying another woman – a woman he had once loved. For a brief instant Rachel experienced a twinge of jealousy.

"Did she hurt you?"

"That kind of wound heals," Grant replied with forced casualness.

"It also leaves a scar," Rachel said. "How deep is yours?"

"Forget it," he snapped. "Another week or two and you'll be well out of it."

Rachel nodded. "Right out of it. As soon as my services can be dispensed with, I'm leaving New Orleans."

"Oh." Grant looked at her in sudden interest. "I thought you might stay here. I could always use you at Sans Souci."

"But not in another capacity." Rachel smiled. "Dear Grant – don't worry about me. I'll manage."

"You're welcome to stay. I owe you a great deal for what you've done here. Weldon was no prize."

"He fulfilled my needs and lined my purse, you both have. Grant –" Green eyes, suddenly grave, searched Grant's face. "Haven't you ever wondered why I left so suddenly?"

"Sometimes, but you know me – I don't press for answers."

"I'd like to tell you."

"Then tell me," Grant replied quietly and moved across beside her on the couch. "Is there some sort of trouble, something I can help out with?"

"Bless you, no. In a way, we're both in the same boat; the only difference is, I have marriage in my future plans."

"Congratulations." Grant showed neither surprise nor amusement.

"Six years ago I came to you without a dollar in the world. You gave me a job and loaned me several hundred dollars unconditionally. No other man I know would have done that."

"I was fascinated by those green eyes," Grant teased. He recalled the incident as if it had been yesterday.

"I was prepared to pay you there and then," Rachel said, meeting his gaze. "You know me, I don't like to owe anything to anyone, but you didn't want me. At least, if you did, I never knew about it."

"You needed a break and I gave it to you. Don't try to make me out a saint, Rachel. We had fun together. What's this about marriage?"

"Do you remember Dave Stanton – no, perhaps not, he drifted into town about the same time you left. He'd followed me through three States."

"A gambler?"

"Far from it, he's a farmer." Rachel met his gaze challengingly. "Go on, laugh, everyone does. How could my kind of woman ever settle down on a dirty farm, they ask? It's simple – I love him. It won't be easy, I'm not fooling myself it will, that's half the battle from the start."

"Does he know you are here?"

"No," Rachel answered. "He's in prison – for manslaughter. He had this little farm his father left him. It was heavily mortgaged and the bank tried to foreclose. Dave had a fight with one of the men who rode out to evict him and killed him. It was an accident."

"And you're waiting for him to be released," Grant said quietly.

"Yes."

"What then?"

Her face brightened. "I have enough money saved for us both to get a new start. We'll buy a small place somewhere and raise our children, like any normal married couple."

"I wish you luck – you deserve it."

Colour mounted beneath the heavy paint on Rachel's cheeks. It was nice to hear a sincere remark from a man.

"You're good for me, Grant – my lucky piece. Since the

day I met you I haven't looked back. When Dave is released next month, I'll be there to meet him, thanks to you – and Ralph Weldon, of course."

"We mustn't forget him, must we?" Grant tucked the wad of bills into an inside pocket. "Why don't you come up to the house for dinner tomorrow?" he asked. "This calls for a celebration."

"I'd like to, but I've already made arrangements to see Ralph. It might look odd if I suddenly put him off, especially if I was seen in Sans Souci. Anyway," her eyes sparkled with amusement, "what would your red-headed lady friend say?"

"Marguerite? We've parted company – this evening, as a matter of fact."

"Have you anyone in mind to take her place?"

"I might have."

"Who are you hurting most by all this – her or yourself?" At her words Grant's face instantly hardened and he rose to his feet.

"It's time I left. Will you still be in town when the house is finished next month?"

"I'll make sure I am. Do I get an invitation to the house-warming?"

"You'll be my guest of honour," Grant promised, and he meant it.

On a cloudy day some six weeks after the funeral of Etienne St. Clair, four large envelopes were hand-delivered to the house on St. George's Avenue. They were addressed to Monsieur and Madame Ralph Weldon, Mademoiselle M. Weldon and Monsieur St. Clair. The fourth envelope was unmarked. It was given into Jemima's hand with instructions that Madame Weldon was to receive it discreetly, without the knowledge of her husband or brother.

The Negress caught sight of Ralph in the doorway of the breakfast room. She handed over three envelopes.

"From the gentleman at Sans Souci. They looked like invitations of some kind."

Marguerite rose from the table and snatched hers from her brother's hand.

"It is from him!" she exclaimed, tearing it open. "Listen to this: 'Monsieur Grant Tyler had pleasure in requesting the company of Miss Marguerite Weldon at the *bal masqué* to be held to celebrate the completion of his new plantation house on the fifteenth September at seven-thirty p.m.' "

Babette stood pale and still at the base of the staircase. Louis had kept her informed of the progress at the house, but she had not expected a lavish opening to mark the occasion.

"A *bal masqué*," Marguerite went on. "How like Grant to think of something like this – even the cream of society will accept his invitations when there is no chance of their being recognised."

Just like it was at the Mardi Gras, Babette thought, and hurriedly sat down beside Louis at the table.

"I think you will find that Monsieur Tyler is no longer an outcast amongst us," his brother said, opening his own invitation. "He has both wealth and place now."

Ralph joined them, frowning deeply. "We are both invited," he said, looking at Babette.

"Do you find it so strange I should be included?" she answered in a perfectly controlled tone. "I am your wife."

"The man forgets you have recently suffered a bereavement," he retorted. "Of course you cannot go. I will send your apologies."

"You will do no such thing!" Louis sprang swiftly to his sister's defence. He could almost read the other man's mind. If Babette did not accompany him, he would be able to take his mistress and no one would know the difference.

He was surprised when Babette laid a hand on his arm.

"He is right, Louis. It is too soon to partake in such a gay affair. I will remain at home."

"September the fifteenth – why, that's only a week from now," Marguerite said. Since parting from Grant they had not encountered each other either at Sans Souci or in the town, although she had contrived many ways to make it possible. His avoidance of her was deliberate, she decided, but here was a chance to resume the acquaintanceship. If he expected her to refuse the invitation he was mistaken. She would attend, suitably masked and wearing the most lavish costume she – or rather Ralph – could afford. She would flirt with him – tease him until he pleaded with her to unmask – then she would reveal herself and dare him to turn his back on her a second time.

Throughout breakfast there was a ceaseless flow of chatter from her and gradually her enthusiasm even reached Ralph. Here was an opportunity to substitute Rachel in his wife's place and flaunt her openly before society. The idea amused him. He knew Rachel would share the joke, and left the house earlier than usual that evening, impatient to break the news to her.

Babette was glad when the initial excitement had died down and the house did not ring with Marguerite's pathetic wail that she would never find a dress in time.

"I'm almost glad I'm not going," Babette said to Jemima as she was preparing for bed.

"It's a shame, that's what it is. Why can't you have fun like everyone else?"

"Hush, we'll have no more of such talk," Babette reproved. "It's too soon for me to come out of mourning."

"A pity others ain't so particular," Jemima sniffed. "Lordy!" In all the excitement and gossip among the servants she had forgotten the envelope tucked in the bosom of her dress. "I was told to give this to you when no one else was around."

Babette's hands were so unsteady that she was forced to hand back the envelope. "Open it for me."

"Well, now, ain't this a coincidence!" Jemima pulled out a gold-edged invitation, just like the others.

"But why send me one separately? Is there a message?"

"It says, 'To a blue-eyed gypsy girl –' "

"Give it to me!" Babette snatched it from her. The words had been written in place of a name and at the bottom of the card she read, "Don't make me come for you. A carriage will call for you at eight p.m."

It was as if he had known she might refuse to accompany Ralph. He expected her to attend unknown to anyone else – and wearing her gypsy costume, as at their first meeting. It was an attempt to humiliate her – to remind her of all that had passed between them.

How vividly that last evening at Sans Souci flooded back to her. She had no choice but to go to the *bal masqué*. She had an understanding with him and it was too late to turn back. What little pride remained forbade her to do so.

"Is there any answer?" Jemima asked curiously.

"No." Babette shook her head. "He knows I will go. This is between us, Jemima, do you understand? On no account must my husband or Mademoiselle Marguerite know. Will you see to my gown for the occasion?"

Jemima's eyes began to start out of her head. "You ain't – you can't go out in that scanty costume again. Not up there –"

"I can and I will. Please do as I say – but make sure it is not seen. Now I'm tired. I am going to bed."

Her authoritative tone put an end to the matter, but it did not prevent Jemima from muttering fervently as she proceeded to brush her young mistress' hair.

"I wish you were coming with us," Louis declared on the evening of the ball.

Babette looked up from her embroidery. They were alone in the drawing room, but she still kept her voice low as she answered, "I am."

"You are – but I thought – does Ralph know?"

"Did he know when I danced as a gypsy girl in the streets?" she returned.

"Not in that costume, *ma petite*," Louis said regarding her seriously. "I forbid it."

"Why not? This is a *bal masqué*. Only you will know my identity."

"And one other. I doubt if you are in any quandary as to whom I refer."

"Actually it was his idea," Babette returned. Her tone was casual, almost light-hearted. It was a brave effort to dispel his fears. Louis had to believe that she was returning to Grant Tyler of her own free will.

"The devil he did!" Louis moved closer to her chair. "So it's true, then. He said you had talked things over between you and resolved your differences. I want to say I'm glad, but at the moment it wouldn't be true. Somehow I can't see you being happy in an illicit love affair, even though he has dispensed with Marguerite's services."

Babette's mouth quivered. "When?"

"Some time ago, I believe. You didn't know?"

"How could I?"

"Marguerite has said nothing? No, perhaps she wouldn't. I dare say her pride has been sorely wounded by our mutual friend. It's not often anyone walks out on the *femme fatale* herself."

"Louis – don't joke about it! I find it shameful."

"And you intend to become his mistress. Or has it happened already?"

"No! Oh no, Louis, you cannot believe that. He has always acted honourably towards me."

Louis' lips twisted in a wry grin. He found it exceedingly hard to believe; only the knowledge of his sister's contempt for lying convinced him. Had Grant Tyler already seduced her, she would have confessed and faced his anger. He was reluctantly forced to accept the fact that she might mean something to the other man after all. He could treat her no worse than Ralph, and if he truly loved her there was still time for Babette's dreams to come true.

"Have you considered the consequences, *mignonne*?"

Babette could not meet his eyes. Yes, she had considered them. They had haunted her through many a sleepless night since Grant had achieved his victory. There was nothing to do except face up to them and put on a brazen attitude before people who had once been her friends. The Big House would become her prison. Inside it she would be safe, but one step outside and she would become swamped by scorn and ridicule.

Grant knew this. In forcing her to go to him, he was openly exposing her to become the number one item of gossip for many months to come. The more she thought of it, the surer she became it was his way of ensuring she remained his until he chose to discard her – as he had so thoughtlessly discarded Marguerite.

Louis sighed at her silence and went upstairs to change. She had not moved from her chair when he reappeared over an hour later – in the costume of a gentleman of Marie Antoinette's court, complete with powdered wig, and silver buckles on his shoes.

"Louis, you look splendid!" Babette gasped. Her embroidery was pushed to one side, forgotten. "I would never have recognised you."

"Ralph and Marguerite put me to shame. Did you see them leave?"

"Ralph, yes. He is in a Mexican costume, is he not?"

"All polished buttons," Louis laughed.

"And what is Marguerite wearing?"

"I've a good mind not to tell you," Louis teased.

"Oh, please! I shall be terrified to go unless I know their costumes in advance."

"Marguerite looks extremely ravishing in black lace and a mantilla."

"A Spanish lady?"

"The same. And now, my little gypsy girl, isn't it time you changed too? Ralph is sending the carriage back for me, but you must have it. I'll walk."

"There is no need. Grant has arranged to have his carriage collect me."

Louis bent forward and kissed her on the cheek.

"Enjoy yourself – but be careful. Should you be recognised it will spoil all future plans."

"Don't worry about me."

"But I do. You are all I have." He drew back, his face breaking into a smile. "Save one dance for me."

"I promise."

Attired in the revealing red dress, her hair loose about her shoulders, Babette stood by the window awaiting the carriage from Sans Souci. The grandfather clock had already chimed the hour, yet there was no sign of it. Was Grant deliberately making it late to unnerve her? She reproved herself strongly for such foolishness, however, as it turned into the courtyard.

With wildly beating heart she sat back in her seat and watched the house disappear behind her. It was too late to turn back now. It had been too late for a long time. With trembling fingers she affixed her velvet mask and sat tensely waiting for Sans Souci to come into view.

Upon entering Sans Souci, Babette immediately searched the sea of costumes, wondering which one hid Grant. She was not kept in suspense for long. While she stood to one side of the room, watching the dancing, he appeared before her, immaculate and disturbingly handsome in evening dress.

"Are you looking for anyone in particular, Blue-eyes?" His voice was so low it did not carry to the next couple.

"I am here. What now?" she answered. There was no friendliness in her voice.

"Why, you must enjoy yourself, of course," Grant said, slipping an arm around her waist. "Come and dance with me."

He guided her into the midst of the dancers, holding her so close that his cheek touched hers.

"Why did you send me a separate invitation?" she asked.

"To make sure you came. I have something important to show you."

"I doubt if there is anything in this house to interest me."

"I shall take great pleasure in proving you wrong. But later, when the party is well under way and we shall not be missed. Is Ralph here?" he asked as his eyes scanned the masked faces around him.

"Yes. He is the Mexican bandit by the punch bowl."

Grant singled him out almost immediately. He smiled slightly at the sight of the blonde-haired woman beside him. Even with her face half hidden, he still recognised Rachel. She had come as she promised, but not as his guest of honour. Instead she had chosen to take Babette's place.

He guessed she was enjoying a last fling among the society of New Orleans before she said goodbye to the old life for ever.

He partnered Babette for several more dances, then left her to mingle with his guests. She continued to find various other partners, but was careful to stay away from Ralph, and was relieved when he escorted his female companion into the garden.

"Exit your main worry," Louis' voice drawled in her ear. "I doubt if we shall see him again for the remainder of the evening."

"Now I can breathe safely," Babette answered. "Once or twice I was sure he was looking straight at me."

"He was probably contemplating seducing you," Louis remarked dryly and his sister shuddered.

"Don't talk that way. What do you think of the new Sans Souci?"

"Monsieur Tyler can be proud of his achievements," he answered, wondering how many rich fools it had needed to provide enough money to buy the two magnificent chandeliers hanging directly above him. He had noticed another in the large hall when he entered.

"Are you admiring my paintings?" Grant came up behind him and followed his gaze. Each side of the marble staircase sweeping upwards to thickly carpeted corridors and softly coloured drapes, were at least a dozen beautifully framed works of art. "Most of them came from France – and a pretty penny they cost me too," he chuckled.

"Are you studying art?" Louis asked with an amused

smile. Grant had long since ceased to amaze him, but it was hard to imagine him as a connoisseur of the arts. It was as if the whole house had been decorated and furnished with one sole purpose in view. To please a woman, perhaps, but was it Babette? "I'm deeply impressed," he added and turned to his sister. "You must invite Monsieur Tyler to inspect our family portraits in father's study, he may find them of interest."

"I doubt it." Babette caught the mockery in Grant's eyes and bit her lips to prevent a further retort.

"You do me an injustice," he murmured. "I believe your husband and I both share the same hobby – we collect beautiful things." He stepped in front of her and offered his arm with a slight bow. "Allow me to show you the rest of my new palace."

When she hesitated, he took her hand and tucked it beneath his arm and smiled disarmingly at Louis.

"Find yourself a pretty girl to dance with, St. Clair, the evening will go quicker," he said lightly, and propelled Babette firmly towards the door.

"Do you want everyone to see us leave?" she protested.

"You were of a mind to disobey me in front of your brother," Grant said coolly. "You should know better."

With a quick glance around him, he ushered her through the french doors into the hall and closed them.

"We'll go through the servants' quarters, in case any inquisitive eyes followed us," he said.

He was thinking of Marguerite in particular. She had made the mistake of wearing a piece of jewellery he had given her not long after they had met. He had recognised her immediately and been amused by her attempts to disguise her voice while she flirted with him. He silently enjoyed the masquerade and played her game to the full.

He led the way down to the servants' quarters. As they entered the kitchen door, a startled Negress spun round from the fire.

Grant's face split into a grin at the sight of the bottle of wine in her hand and the two glasses on the table in front of his manservant, Sam.

"It's a good vintage – enjoy it while you can," he chuckled, "but be sure to leave enough for upstairs!"

"You treat your people well," Babette said as she preceded him along the passage towards the back staircase.

"Why shouldn't I? They are human beings."

"I was about to say, you treat them better than Louis or myself."

Grant's dark eyes rested on her face.

"Jemima has never tried to shoot me, and Sam has never challenged me to a duel. Does that answer your question?"

"Have you ever tried to make Jemima your mistress?" she retorted with cheeks flaming.

"Touché," Grant murmured. "I admit I have not." He opened a door and led her into the other part of the house. Before them stretched a long corridor covered in a deep magenta-coloured carpet.

"This part of the house is private," Grant said quietly. "I thought you would prefer it that way,"

"I – !" Babette repeated amazed.

"Of course. These are your apartments," he answered.

CHAPTER
NINE

THE bedroom in which Babette stood was decorated in the most beautiful shade of pastel blue. Everything was varying shades of blue, from the velvet drapes at the french window to the embroidered coverlets embossed with gold and the plain carpet beneath her feet. A pair of cherubs hovered over the magnificent four-poster bed in the centre of the room. The sheets and pillow-cases, even the toilet requisites on the Louis XVI dressing-table were enbroidered with a large letter "B" in gold thread.

"I trust they meet with your approval," Grant said.

"I am surprised you afford me such luxury." Babette tried to sound aloof, but failed. She was too taken aback.

"I shall be repaid. Come, let me finish the guided tour." Besides the bedroom there was an exquisite bathroom with a sunken marble bath and a small dressing-room where, he informed her, Jemima could sleep if he was ever away from the house all night.

"Do you intend moving from Sans Souci?" Babette asked, following him into the sitting-room. This was in pastel grey, tastefully picked out in gold, as were the other rooms. All the chairs, and the couch, were covered in a deep burgundy brocade. There were bookshelves lined with books of every description, a framed landscape picture hung on the largest wall, and there was even a small piano. He did not intend her to grow bored, she realised.

"As soon as I've found someone to manage Sans Souci for me I'll move in here. Until then you can stay where you are. No need to start the gossips talking yet."

His reference to gossips brought Babette back to reality

with a sickening thud. For a moment the splendour of her surroundings had dazzled her and made her forget that in a very short while she was to become Grant's mistress.

She looked at the harsh line of his mouth which had once plied her own with gentle, persuasive kisses – the lean, finely boned face, bronzed, unsmiling. She had known it to bear the kindest of smiles. And those black eyes had not always looked at her so coldly. Once they had looked at her and she had felt a woman. Now she was too numb to feel anything.

She would come to this fine house when he sent for her, and she would live with him, regardless of any gossip or any action on the part of her husband. She had no choice, but that was only part of it. She still loved him. When he found she was willing to stay, he might even be civil to her, but he would never again believe she loved him, and that was the bitterest pill of all.

She sat down while Grant went across to the decanter and glasses on the sideboard and poured out drinks for them both.

"We ought to drink a toast," he said as he handed her a glass.

"To what – your great victory? I hope you find I am worth it."

Grant's face hardened. He didn't want a quarrel. He wanted her to accept things for what they were and make it easier for them both.

"You will be wise to remember you are bought and paid for," he returned cruelly, "and I like my investments to be repaid at least double."

Babette blanched and her hand trembled as she sipped the sweet sherry. It was useless to retaliate.

Leaning forward, he unfastened her mask and drew it off.

"Someone may come in," Babette protested.

"No one will come to this part of the house," he assured her. "We are quite safe."

"Your guests will be noticing your absence." Babette

caught her breath at the intentness of his gaze. She had seen such a longing before – when they had met openly for the first time by the bayou and she had lain in his arms while they planned their future. Was it possible that some feeling for her still lingered beneath the hatred and contempt?

"Are we in agreement, Blue-eyes?" He set her glass aside and caught her chin between firm fingers, turning her face to him.

"What do you want me to say?" she breathed.

"That you will come to me when I send for you. If I should have to fetch you it may turn into something of a spectacle."

"I shall come – only –"

"Only – what? There are no complications."

"Have you forgotten my husband? He will not stand by while I leave him to go to another man."

A smile touched Grant's lean mouth.

"He is no problem, as I've told you before. By the time you come here, I shall have dealt with him."

Babette was silent. She had no doubt Ralph would employ some devious tactics before he came to heel, and she found herself wishing it was all over.

Grant looked down at her face, half hidden against his coat. He too was remembering that day by the bayou. It had haunted him unceasingly – a reminder of how foolish a man becomes when his senses are dulled by love. He was older and wiser now, and Babette was still beside him. Without warning he bent and kissed her. She stiffened and tried to twist away. Angrily he caught her to him and kissed her unwilling mouth until it was no longer unwilling and she no longer fought him.

"By all accounts you have missed my kisses," he mocked, drawing back. "Has Ralph never given you a man's kiss?"

Bright tears flooded into Babette's eyes. She had been shaken out of all composure.

"He does not have your talents," she answered in a scarcely audible voice.

"Then you will not miss him, will you?"

"If you mean to take me now, do so, but don't torture me," she begged. "I can't stand it."

Her distress was genuine, not merely a show for sympathy, Grant thought and felt a momentary twinge of compassion. Releasing her, he stood up.

"I've waited long enough for you," he said gruffly. "A few more days won't harm me."

Was it only to be days? Babette thought sitting upright. So soon – yet she had been expecting a summons since the night her father died.

Grant watched her wipe away the last traces of tears and stand up, not very steadily. He picked up her mask and affixed it in place, conscious of uncertainty in her eyes. Cupping her face in his hands he kissed her for the last time. It was a long, soul-searching kiss that succeeded in evoking more from him than he had intended. Babette trembled against him, but made no attempt to pull away.

"To tide you over until we are together," he murmured. "Shall we rejoin our guests?"

As they came out of the apartments and turned towards the back staircase, Grant halted her abruptly. At the top of the stairs another figure had appeared and was heading in their direction. He needed only a single glance to recognise Marguerite.

Quickly he pushed Babette back into the room and closed the doors.

"Your sister-in-law," he said with a tight smile. "I'm not sure, but I think she may have seen us."

"Does it matter? She will know soon enough in any case."

"Would you prefer it to be tonight with the house full of prominent people?" Grant retorted. "Give me credit for a little feeling. As long as you play fair with me, I'll try to shield you as much as possible." Taking her hand he led her into the sitting-room and through a communicating door which led into another bedroom. Before Babette had time for questions, they were passing into various other rooms.

"In case you were wondering, they were my rooms, of

course," Grant said as they came out on to the wide landing overlooking the ballroom.

"Why didn't you just put bars on the doors of my apartment?" Babette asked bitterly.

"I have no fear you will try to leave," he answered. "There is nowhere you could go."

Ahead of them the corridor was empty but he knew that any moment Marguerite would be coming around a corner to confront them.

"Go down to the kitchen and tell Sam he is to drive you home," he ordered, guiding Babette towards the staircase.

"Louis can take me –"

"He will be missed. Do as you are told. I'll be in touch with you."

Grant leant over the balustrade and watched her hurry downstairs, threading her way through the dancers to the door. Amid so many bright colours her dress was unnoticeable. He breathed a sigh of relief. Hearing a rustle of skirt behind him, he turned to face Marguerite.

"You are seeking someone?" he asked smilingly.

Marguerite halted beside him and looked down into the ballroom.

"I was admiring your magnificent house," he answered.

"Are you sure you weren't following me, Maggie?"

"You know! Oh, how could you?"

Grant touched the glittering bracelet on her left wrist.

"You should have chosen your jewellery with more care. I gave this to you – or have you had so many presents from male admirers you've forgotten which is which?"

Marguerite had forgotten, and her annoyance grew.

"Who was that with you?" She tried in vain to pick out a gypsy girl below and wondered if he had left her to hide in one of the rooms.

"Was anyone with me?"

"I followed you when you left, but Louis detained me and the wretched man made me dance with him. She is wearing the costume of a gypsy."

"How intriguing," Grant murmured. By now Sam would be driving Babette home. He could let Marguerite prattle on without fear of his secret becoming known.

"Grant – who is she?"

"How could I know – she was masked. We played an amusing little game. She told my fortune and in return I allowed her to keep her identity."

"What piece of jewellery did you give her to mark such an auspicious occasion?" Marguerite asked spitefully.

"She isn't in this for gain."

"For love then – so that's it." Marguerite stepped back, staring at him. "She is the one, isn't she? The other woman."

Grant regarded her with an amused smile. After a moment he nodded. There was no harm in her knowing, he decided, and it might help to keep her out of his way.

"Do you like my new home?" he asked, when she remained silent.

"Is it for her?"

"Of course –"

"She has expensive tastes." Marguerite could not suppress the envy from her voice. All this could have been hers if she had learned to control her greed. Now it belonged to another woman – an unnamed shadow who appeared and disappeared without a trace. She wanted to see her and make comparisons.

"When do you intend to bring her here?"

"Soon – very soon." Grant straightened and lighted a cheroot. "Your curiosity is insatiable, my dear, you must learn to curb it. The name of my future wife is no concern of yours."

So he was to take a wife! Marguerite racked her brains as she had done so often before in an attempt to put a name to his mysterious companion. She knew every eligible girl in New Orleans. None of them would fit the description of the gypsy girl. Petite and dark, with an attractive figure. There were many dark women in the town. She could be any one of a dozen unmarried girls, or any one of a dozen more who were married – or widowed.

"Why don't you forget about her and enjoy yourself," Grant said quietly. "Everyone else is. By the way, I have some business to discuss with your brother. Point him out to me, will you?"

Marguerite stared at the costumed figures.

"There – the tall Mexican bandit. Aren't you going down?" she asked suspiciously when he did not move. Did he want her to rejoin the others, leaving him free to go back to his mistress?

"In a moment, when he has finished his drink. I must admit I would not have recognised him – nor Mrs. Weldon. They make a striking pair, don't you think?"

Marguerite began to laugh. "A striking pair indeed, only that's not my sister-in-law. She's still at home, mourning her beloved father. Ralph took this opportunity to amuse himself at your expense."

"I see. I take it Mrs. Weldon is not aware of her husband's – philanderings."

"Of course she is. Ralph doesn't keep it a secret from her. Why should he? When a wife even keeps her favours from her husband, it's only natural he should seek satisfaction elsewhere."

Unaware of the sudden hardening of Grant's expression she picked up her skirts and proceeded downstairs.

Babette was awakened by the sound of someone swearing blindly outside the bedroom door. She sat bolt upright, shivering in the keenness of early morning air. She had no doubt as to who it was outside, but it had been so long since Ralph had tried to force an entry into her room, she hoped he had given up.

"Babette – open the door. It's Ralph – your husband." His voice was slurred with drink, so that the words were rolled into each other. "Be a good girl and let me in."

"Go away or I'll call Louis," Babette said firmly. Struggling into a wrap, she sat tensely on the edge of the bed.

"He isn't here." There was a chuckle which sent a shiver of fear down her spine. "He's still at the party. C'mon – little wife – let me in."

She did not answer. A silence ensued, then suddenly the door shuddered under a fierce blow.

"If you won't open it – I'll break it down!" Ralph shouted. "Damn you, I've stood enough! I'll show you how to be warm! I'll make you want me – love me. You'll see – it won't be so hard once you learn how."

Babette pressed her hands over her ears to shut out his wild babblings. If Louis had not yet returned to the house there would only be the servants. Wheeling about, she ran to the bell-rope and tugged at it furiously.

While she stood trembling in the middle of the room, she heard Marguerite's furious tones. Jemima's voice joined in until there was such a babble of voices she could not distinguish any one clearly.

"Make him go away, Jemima." She leant against the door, her face pressed to the wooden panels. "Fetch Jason, anything, but make him go away!"

"Don't worry – he's on his way," came the answer from Marguerite.

Babette heard more footsteps on the landing and Jason talking quietly to those outside. Then someone heaved a sigh of relief.

"You can open the door now," Marguerite said. "It's safe. Tell her, Jemima."

"He's gone, Missy – honest to God – he's gone."

Slowly Babette unlocked the door and inched it open. "I thought he would break it down," she said weakly.

"We all did." Marguerite was still in her masquerade gown. She had been escorted home by a young and very pleasant Naval lieutenant and had been lingering in the driveway when Ralph's carriage almost bowled them over. "My brother has had a rather unpleasant interview with Grant Tyler," she added.

"Did he say why?"

"Apparently Monsieur Tyler is concerned at the amount of money he is owed – at least that's the story Ralph told me. He's being pressed for payment. It's odd – debts have never worried him before. He can borrow it on his share of the St. Clair Line – yet he's acting like a mad bear. I've never seen him quite this way before –" She broke off, staring at her sister-in-law.

There was no light in Babette's room and she stood in the shadowy half-light thrown by the lamp Jemima was holding. Her hair was loose about her shoulders, her silk wrap hanging loosely open.

An image presented itself in Marguerite's mind – the wild, exotic image of a gypsy girl.

"Is anything wrong?" Babette asked. She stepped forward out of the darkness and immediately the spell was broken.

Marguerite inwardly laughed at such a ridiculous suspicion and dismissed it.

"You look very pale, Jemima had better stay with you until morning," she answered solicitously.

Babette nodded. She welcomed the idea of the Negress' protection while she slept, and allowed herself to be fussed over and put to bed without a single word of protest.

As she settled beneath the covers once more she wondered at the real reason for Ralph's visit to Grant. Was it only to discuss money – or something far more important?

Ralph was not at all pleased by the letter he received from Grant Tyler the following morning.

". . . further to our conversation of last night, unless the full amount of the I.O.U.s held here are redeemed within three days, further action will be taken. . ."

Three days! It was impossible to find the money in that time.

There was no answer to his insistent hammering on Babette's door, and at length he opened it and went in. The room was empty. He went straight to the jewel box on her dressing-table and emptied the contents into his handker-chief.

Hurrying out to the stables, he ordered a horse to be saddled. While he was waiting he noticed that Babette's horse was missing from its stall, but he paid little attention to the fact – he was far too anxious to reach Sans Souci and fling her jewellery into Grant's face.

Beneath the trees along the Bayou St. Michael, Babette tethered her horse and walked along the sandy beach. It had been weeks since she had enjoyed an early morning ride. Beyond the ridge lay the plantations and the Big House, but she kept well out of sight. She would be able to ride that way soon enough. Once the wagging tongues began she would probably be glad of its isolation from the rest of the town. She had almost accepted the inevitable, except for one disturbing factor. Once Ralph discovered where she was and why, nothing would prevent him from spreading the St. Clair scandal throughout New Orleans. Doubtless he would enjoy it, she thought bitterly. He would be humiliating her for the non-consummation of their marriage and ruining Louis whom he hated.

She paused to throw some pebbles into the calm waters. How easy it was to feel at peace in this place, undisturbed by the outside world.

As she turned back to where her horse was tethered, a rider cantered into view along the top of the bank. Instinctively she ducked behind a tree, but as the strains of a French folk tune reached her ears, she hurried out into the open.

"Louis – *viens ici. C'est* Babette."

Her brother reined in and waited for her to remount and join him.

"What on earth are you doing out at this ungodly hour?" he asked with a broad smile.

"I was hoping to see you."

"You are lucky to catch me, *ma petite*. Grant and I are just on our way back to breakfast."

"Grant! Oh, no, I don't want to see him now." But it was too late. Even as she spoke he came galloping across from the direction of the plantations.

"Hasn't anyone been to bed yet?" he asked gazing at Babette.

"I came out here before the rest of the house was awake," Babette replied. "You know I enjoy to ride in the early morning."

"Indeed I do. In the near future we shall be able to enjoy it together, shan't we?"

Louis glanced at his sister enquiringly, only to find her gaze averted.

"Is there something I should know?"

"Haven't you told him yet?" Grant asked Babette.

"No – I –"

"Then I suggest now is a good time – at least over breakfast. I also have something to say to Louis which I think you should hear. It will save complications arising. Shall we go back to Sans Souci?"

His tone left no room for argument. Babette turned her horse about and the others followed suit.

Solicitously Grant helped her to dismount before the stables and put an arm around her waist as they waited for Louis to join them.

"There is no need for such pretence," Babette said in a fierce whisper.

"Oh, but there is." Grant's smiling face looked down into her angry one. "Louis must be made to believe that whatever is done in the future is of your own free will. That you decided it because you are unhappy with Weldon and still deliriously in love with me. Don't give him reason to think otherwise – it would make me very angry. I like your brother – we are friends. Don't try to get at me through him."

"Why should I not play your game?" Babette retorted. "You used him to hurt me."

"And succeeded – that was before I really knew him,"

Grant answered seriously. "I wouldn't like him to be a pawn again."

The three of them went upstairs to the breakfast room where Grant's housekeeper was setting out platefuls of food which smelt deliciously appetising.

"I seed you a-coming," she said cheerfully.

"Remind me to raise your wages," Grant said, settling Babette in a chair at the table.

Babette stared across the table at Grant in wide-eyed surprise. Not only was he ignoring the snobbish upper class conventions of the New Orleans aristocracy by daring to set himself up in their midst as a landowner, but he actually made no secret of the fact that he paid wages to his coloured workers! They were slaves – bought and paid for, no doubt, from profits reaped from the gaming tables of Sans Souci! Was he trying to antagonise the whole world against him with such audacious and unheard-of behaviour? No one paid wages to slaves – at least not here in New Orleans, and as he intended to make his home here and continue running a profitable business, he would do well to remember it. She would have Louis speak to him – tactfully, of course.

"How about mine?" Louis grinned. "Then I might have enough to pay you what I owe you."

"How much is it now?" Grant asked, seating himself and eyeing with relish the large plate of fried tomatoes, eggs, bacon and bread the Negress placed before him. She quickly attended to the others and then left them alone.

"A couple of hundred, I think – certainly not much more," Louis answered after a moment's calculation. "I was lucky on the tables last week."

"Take over Sans Souci for me, and we'll call it quits," Grant murmured with a sidelong glance at Babette.

Louis almost choked over a piece of bacon.

"Take over – here? As manager? What about the plantation?"

"Find someone else. Of course the job isn't the kind I

should offer to a St. Clair, neither was that of overseer, but you're a damned good one."

Louis looked suspiciously at his sister. "Has this anything to do with you?"

"In a way I suppose it has." Babette only picked at her food. Her appetite had suddenly vanished. She managed to meet his gaze and hold it. "Grant wants to move into the Big House as soon as possible, but he can't unless there is someone here to run Sans Souci."

"What she's trying to say is that I want more time – more free time. Once I'm in the other house I don't intend to keep running backwards and forwards to settle petty disputes. You can do that – you've proved you're capable and besides people know and will trust you – probably far more than they do me."

Louis chuckled.

"The idea appeals to me. Can you see Ralph's face when I refuse him credit?"

"I doubt if he'll be coming here much longer." Grant helped himself to another two rashers of bacon and two eggs with a slow smile.

"I hear you are pressing for payment," Louis said, wishing he had been present last night at the encounter between Grant and his brother-in-law.

"He has three days. Didn't he show you my letter?" Grant asked Babette.

"I told you. I came out before he was up."

"Of course." He turned to his food with a frown. He had never understood why Babette's bedroom was on one side of the house and her husband's on the other. However, it didn't matter now. It would be different at the Big House, for he and she would share adjoining apartments. She would be there whenever he wanted her. He found it strange that he could not visualise what it would be like.

"If I accept your offer," Louis said, leaning across the table towards him, "it would mean I live here?"

"What else?"

"Unfortunately that's the one snag."

Babette laid down her knife and fork and pushed the plate to one side. He was considering her. Dear Louis – thoughtful to the last. Forcing a smile to her lips, she said in a very controlled tone, "Don't worry about me, *mon frère*. You see, as soon as Grant finds someone to take over from him, he moves to the Big House. I shall be joining him. I am leaving Ralph."

CHAPTER
TEN

BABETTE'S news did not cause such a commotion as she expected; in fact Louis showed hardly any surprise. It was as if he had been waiting for such an announcement.

"Babette is under the impression you will be against it," Grant said quietly, when Louis remained silent. He was inclined to agree with her.

"I am against anything which will hurt my sister," the other replied at length. "This may at first, but in the long run I know it will be the best thing she has ever done." He smiled reassuringly at Babette and reached across the table to squeeze her hand. "I knew you two were up to something – the house was a dead give-away."

"Only one thing worries me," Babette began. Louis silenced her with a frown.

"I can take care of Ralph. I understand what could happen, but it won't. There is always the river."

"It would probably spit him back at you," Grant said cheerfully. "I understand your first misgivings were a natural concern for your sister, but now she has told you of our plans, I think we should go into more details, don't you? I want you to know exactly what it will mean to take over Sans Souci – what kind of opposition you will be up against – although I suspect you have already worked that out for yourself. Why don't we go into the other room where we can relax and be more comfortable?"

And that was that, Babette thought as she rose and followed him into the drawing room. How calmly she was abiding by his set of rules – even her lies to Louis were bold with conviction. Were they lies? Wasn't she glad to be leaving Ralph and Marguerite and the house her brother had always regarded as a graveyard? All her unhappy memories could be left there too. Once she went to Grant he would be her whole life; only Louis visiting them from Sans Souci would be her one source of reality and a link with the past.

"You aren't angry with me now?" She turned apprehensively to face her brother.

"Not if it means you will be happy." His eyes searched her face. How easy it would be to blurt out the truth while he was not looking at her, compelling her to go on with this act. She swallowed hard and said, "If it didn't do you think I would run the gauntlet against the whole town? Will you accept Grant's offer now, Louis? Please say yes, then my happiness is complete."

She sounded so carefree that Grant wheeled around to look at her, and his heart lurched unsteadily at the half-smile on her face. A word, a smile, a look from those blue eyes – he was beginning to be affected again.

How was she managing it? Last night he had kissed her to prove that everything he had once felt for her was dead; instead he had aroused a nagging suspicion in the depths of him that he was not as invulnerable as he wanted to believe. She had tried to fight against him and failed – and he had found it still pleasant to hold her in his arms and forget the past and her treachery.

"I think it will be a great deal easier to say yes here and now and let you two love-birds finish making your plans," Louis said and warmly shook Grant's outstretched hand. "You know I'm grateful, and not only for the job."

"Forget it." Grant pulled free, oddly disturbed by the other man's sincerity. "You can move in here as soon as you like, there are plenty of bedrooms. We can go over the books together and clear up various other matters." He broke off as there came a knock on the door, followed by the appearance of Sam's worried features.

"Mr. Weldon is on his way up, Massa Grant. I tried to stop him, but he insisted he couldn't wait."

Grant caught Babette's arm and pushed her towards the other room.

"Stay out of sight," he warned.

Louis came up behind them and handed her her purse.

"We don't want to make him unduly suspicious, do we?" he said with a smile. Then to Grant. "Do you want me to stay?"

"You may find yourself dealing with him in the future – come and learn how to play dirty," Grant answered, firmly closing the communicating door. When Ralph was shown into the room, they were both standing by the fire, poring over a large ledger.

"I have something for you, Tyler," Ralph said harshly, and had pulled the handkerchief containing Babette's jewels from his pocket before he became aware of the other man's presence.

"What's he doing here?"

"Monsieur St. Clair has just accepted management of Sans Souci," Grant replied coolly, closing the ledger and putting it to one side. "Won't you sit down, Weldon? A cup of coffee, perhaps, you look as if you've had a hard ride."

Ralph's face was extremely red and he was breathing heavily. The gaze of Louis' narrowed grey eyes on him was adding to his discomfort. He had tramped all over town trying to borrow money – with little success. No one had wanted to know him once he had ventured on the subject. Perhaps Babette's jewellery could buy him time. Contemptuously he flung the folded handkerchief on to the table.

"How much will you give me for those, damn you?"

Grant motioned to Louis.

"Your first chance at diplomacy," he murmured. "See if you can accommodate our friend."

The smile faded from his face as Louis bent and uncovered the shimmering cluster of stones.

"Babette's jewels," Louis gasped. "Where did you get these?" he demanded of Ralph.

"She gave them to me, of course, like an obedient wife

trying to help her husband out of a little financial difficulty," came the smooth reply.

"You are a liar," Louis snapped. "When did she give them to you?"

Ralph's mouth tightened.

"Your new position has gone to your head, St. Clair. It was this morning if you must know."

"I met my sister not an hour ago," Louis said coldly. "She left the house before anyone was up. If you'd taken her jewels she would have told me. Most of them belonged to our mother; nothing in the world would induce her to part with them."

Except to help you, Grant thought to himself. He knew Ralph had taken them without Babette's knowledge or permission, and he felt anger rise inside him at such a cold-blooded theft. It would give him great satisfaction to watch this man crawl. Casually he examined a pair of diamond clasps. He had seen those before, and the emerald necklace Louis was holding.

"They are worth very little to me," he said. "No more than fifteen hundred."

"Why, you!" Ralph started forward menacingly.

"Perhaps you can get more elsewhere," Grant snapped. "If so don't waste my time and your own – you have little of it left."

"What do you want from me?" Ralph demanded. "You own the house I live in, you are my business partner, you amuse yourself with my sister until she bores you, and then you throw her aside."

"I'll have to be careful or I shall soon be down to your level," Grant replied. "Have you anything else to discuss, Weldon? We are in the middle of something important."

"I'll be back," Ralph said hoarsely.

"Be sure and bring some money with you."

The loud slamming of the door after Ralph's departing figure almost drowned Grant's mocking reply.

Babette came slowly out of the other room, her eyes fixed

on the necklace he was holding. Ralph had ransacked her jewel casket – everything she owned was on the table. She noticed none of Marguerite's precious pieces were there. Her wily sister-in-law had probably locked everything away just in case. How well she knew her brother!

"You didn't give them to him, did you?" Louis asked gently.

"Of course she didn't," Grant retorted.

"You seem very sure."

"I am. Once upon a time your sister tried to sell me her jewels to pay some of your debts. I refused them. She'd hardly try to make me take them a second time."

Dropping the emeralds into the handkerchief, he fastened it together and held it out to her. "Put these in a safe place where Weldon's prying hands can't get at them."

"But – but they are in lieu of what he owes you," she said faintly.

"They are your property," Grant said roughly, and abruptly turned away. He was being weak again. He should have kept the jewellery and sold it in order to compensate some of his losses. Instead he had returned it to her like a real Southern gentleman.

Babette stood motionless, lost for words while Louis stared at her, then at Grant, puzzled by her strange reaction.

"I seem to be in the way," he said, his face clearing. Of course, she was waiting to be alone with Grant.

"There'll be time for sentiment later," Grant said, re-opening the ledger. "Will you excuse us, Babette, we have business to discuss."

Louis escorted her to the door, his eyes twinkling.

"Why don't we invite Monsieur Tyler to dinner this evening, to celebrate?" he murmured.

"Why – yes – if he'll come," Babette replied after a slight hesitation.

"You will, won't you?" Louis asked turning to his employer.

"Don't you think I've provoked Weldon enough! Let's

have dinner together by all means, but here at Sans Souci where we can enjoy our meal without fear of interruption, then afterwards perhaps we can go down to the tables. As far as I know Babette has never tried her luck on them."

Babette looked to her brother for guidance. People would talk if she came out of mourning so soon. Louis nodded his approval.

"It will be quite an experience," he laughed.

One she would not forget in a hurry, Babette thought. Tonight she would know whether or not she had the necessary courage to face the months ahead.

"I'm glad to see you are not wearing black," Louis said when he came to collect her. "That blue gown is very attractive."

"I was afraid you wouldn't approve," Babette answered.

"This morning you proved to me what a sensible young woman you are. At the moment I approve of everything," Louis assured her.

Babette was aware of many curious eyes turned in her direction as she entered Sans Souci. Forcing a smile to her lips, she made her way past the crowded tables, acknowledging many familiar faces with a slight nod or a brief word. Louis caught up with her on the stairs, took her hand, and laid it on his arm with a grin. "Well done, little one."

The worst was yet to come, Babette thought. A visit to Sans Souci, escorted by her brother, was permissible – but to appear in public with Grant Tyler as her companion and to gamble at the tables was something completely different. By morning she would be the most talked-about woman in town. A brazen hussy who put aside her mourning dress for the bright lights of Sans Souci and undesirable company.

Grant greeted them in the drawing room, and after an aperitif, they sat down to dinner. The marvellous meal was washed down with a magnum bottle of champagne.

"We are celebrating," Grant said smiling when Louis asked the reason for such a sumptuous spread.

"Originally you were invited to dine with us."

Grant shrugged his shoulders carelessly. He was in a good mood and the best part of the evening was yet to come.

"When you are installed here, Babette and I will come to visit you," he answered. "By then you may have found yourself a wife – or something." A strange look flickered in Louis' eyes as Grant eyed him amusedly. "Doesn't the idea appeal to you? I'm surprised, St. Clair, I never took you for a lone wolf. Or do you have a nice little Creole girl tucked away somewhere?"

Louis turned pale. Grant flashed a quick look at Babette and saw that she, too, was colourless. He had touched on a raw spot for them both. Could whatever it was be the reason why she had married Weldon? Had she told him the truth and deliberately turned her back on love to shield her family? He felt himself grow cold at the thought. If it was true there was no justification for the way he had treated her.

"I apologise for my bad taste in jokes," he said quietly and rose to his feet. "Shall we enjoy our coffee in the other room before we go downstairs?"

Louis nodded and smiled, his moment of discomfort passing.

Babette tried to exclude herself from the conversation, but Grant would not allow it, determined her brother should discover nothing amiss between them. He was pleased she had decided to come out of mourning, yet surprised she had chosen this particular evening to do so. He remembered the jewel case in his desk and smiled to himself. Now was as good a time as any.

Babette looked at him in silent amazement as he took the case from a drawer and opened it in front of her. The sight of the magnificent sapphire pendant took her breath away.

"I chose it because it matches your eyes," he murmured.

"You bought it – for me?"

"By her reaction, you'd think she was the first woman ever to receive a present from the man who loves her," Louis laughed.

Grant's mouth twisted slightly, but he made no comment.

Lifting the pendant from its bed of midnight blue velvet, he carefully fastened it around Babette's throat.

"It does match your eyes," he said, stepping back.

Babette touched the cold stone nestling above her breast – still too surprised to speak. Grant leaned down and kissed her briefly on the lips. It was the finishing touch to the happy impression he had created in Louis' mind.

"Shall we try our luck at the tables?" he asked.

"I should leave this here for safety." Babette touched the sapphire, her eyes appealing to Grant. If Ralph is here, how shall I explain it to him in front of everyone? they asked.

"Are you suggesting my clientele are not of the highest social standing, Blue-eyes?"

He was determined she should wear it, Babette realised, and did not press the matter further.

The lower floor of Sans Souci was crowded with people, probably attracted by the two new tables he had installed, Grant told them. Babette saw her brother's eyes light up.

"Do you never grow tired of it?" she asked softly as he steered them in the direction of the new tables.

"Louis and I both have gambling fever in our blood," Grant said, lighting a cheroot.

"And when Babette chooses to be reckless, she is almost uncontrollable," Louis chuckled.

Grant motioned to the dealer that he would take over.

"Then I suggest now is the time for her to be reckless – as you put it."

"The stakes are far too high for me," Babette replied, hanging back.

"The House will cover your losses – if you lose," Grant said, pulling out a chair for her. "Sit down and try your luck."

Louis sat on one side of her, Grant stood on the other handling the cards. Babette allowed her brother to peer over her shoulder and dictate how she should play. To her surprise she found she won. As a large amount of chips were pushed her way for the third time, she looked up at Grant, suspecting him of arranging her windfall. He was concentrating on shuffling the cards.

"Do you want to change your chips?" he asked, without glancing up.

"Of course not," Louis answered in disgust. "The way she's winning?"

Grant's eyes met Babette's. In them she saw the reason for her good fortune – she had been right. The cards had been dealt the way he wanted them.

"Perhaps I should, Louis –" she began.

"It's always wise not to overplay your hand," Grant remarked quietly, "I think I told you that once before."

His words jarred Babette. He was making it impossible for them to be together without an argument, deliberately goading her – knowing full well she could not cause a scene with so many people around.

"Louis is right, I will go on." Bravely she returned his challenging gaze. Do your worst, her eyes said silently. You cannot hurt me any more than you have. "It's your money anyway," she added.

Grant gave a tight smile and flickered a card towards her. She sat back and looked at it, the Queen of Hearts. Beside her Louis gave a soft whistle.

"I wonder what a certain person would make of this?" he muttered.

Babette caught her breath. He was holding the Ace of Spades – the death card. Once there had been in Louis' life a young girl who had amused him by telling his fortune by the cards. She had believed in their powers, and although Louis had laughed at first, at length he too had not scoffed at her readings. They had had the uncanny knack of coming true. She had even foretold her own death. He looked into his sister's worried face and smiled.

"Superstitious nonsense," he said firmly. He picked up the remainder of his cards and the incident was closed, having passed unnoticed by all except Grant.

Since his encounter with Grant earlier that day, Ralph's temper had not improved. He sought solace with Rachel, hoping to spend the last few hours with her, before she boarded the river steamer, and had been wild with anger when she refused to see him. An attempt to force an entry had resulted in him being escorted firmly out of the front door by a Negro servant.

He saw his hopes of paying off his debts fading rapidly into the distance when he began to lose heavily at the poker tables. Across from him Marguerite stood behind a good-looking young officer, who was her constant escort of late. He was winning, and she would reap the benefit from him. Her nest was safely lined.

His lips tightened. It was no use to go to his wife, she had no money and no jewels. Damn Tyler and his infernal gambling house, he thought.

A crowd was gathering around the roulette wheel and Marguerite's companion raised his head in interest.

"Someone seems to be lucky."

"That makes two of you," Ralph growled. He slammed his useless cards down on to the table and pushed back his chair. "Perhaps some of it will brush off on me."

Marguerite leaned forward and selected several chips. "I'll pay you back," she murmured, lightly touching her companion's cheek, and hurried after her brother.

"I don't want your charity," Ralph snarled as she pressed them into his hand.

"I'd take them if I were you, they could multiply."

"Your generosity amazes me –"

"I don't want you to make a scene," Marguerite began and then she broke off, her eyes fixed on the young girl with the mound of chips before her. She tugged at Ralph's sleeve.

"Am I seeing things? It's Babette – and she's winning. Your luck has changed."

Ralph stared at Babette, but his interest was not centred on her winnings. He was fascinated by the sapphire pendant around her neck.

"Where did she get that?"

"What?"

"The pendant. Damn you, look at it. I've never seen it before."

"Perhaps it was a present from her ex-lover, before you married her."

"If it was I'd have found it when I –" Ralph did not finish. If Marguerite knew he had taken Babette's jewellery, she would hide her own and that was his last chance. "Never mind."

Marguerite moved closer, jealousy studying her sister-in-law and wondering what man in his right mind would give such a dazzling jewel to such a dull, uninteresting person.

"How convenient to have your brother working for the owner," Ralph sneered. His remark was deliberately loud and the people clustered round the tables heard it. Conversation ceased abruptly – as everyone waited for some reaction from Grant.

There was very little. Even Louis expected a show of anger, but there was none. Grant did not look up for a long moment, then he turned to face Ralph, a contemptuous twist to his mouth.

"Have you been losing again?" he inquired, "or are you merely annoyed because someone is having a lucky win?"

"Luck has nothing to do with it," Ralph returned heavily.

"Is that meant to insinuate I'm dealing from the bottom of the deck?" Grant's eyes darkened. With deliberate slowness he rose to his feet and put down the deck of cards he was holding.

"Ralph – are you out of your mind?" Marguerite caught his arm. "Please, excuse him, Grant – he has not been himself tonight," she said, with forced sweetness.

"I suggest you take him home," Grant replied coolly. He was determined not to be drawn into an argument – Babette's presence made him too vulnerable.

"I suggest you allow someone else to deal," Ralph blurted

out. The sapphire at his wife's throat swam before his eyes, infuriating him beyond all reasonable control.

Babette stiffened and reached for Louis' hand. "He's mad," she whispered. "What is he trying to do?"

Louis shook his head, not replying.

"Bring me a new deck," Grant ordered coldly. "Jimmie – come here."

The dealer at the poker table rose and came to his side. Grant motioned to the fresh pack of cards, and moved away to stand behind Louis' chair.

Babette's hands trembled as she reached for her cards. What had Grant been thinking of to hand over so meekly? He had been allowing her to win, now she must surely lose and prove Ralph right – Sans Souci would be ruined. She cast a desperate glance over her shoulder, but he was not even looking at her. With her last hand, she became reckless and pushed all her chips into the centre of the table – anxious to have done with it. She almost fainted when she won.

A murmur of approval ran from the onlookers. Someone said something to Grant which made him burst into laughter. "I trust you are satisfied," he said across the table to Ralph. "Perhaps now the evening can continue in peace." He motioned forward a uniformed Negro. "Have Mrs. Weldon's chips cashed. Yours too, St. Clair?"

"Yes, I've had enough for tonight. I need a drink," Louis said, mopping his brow. "Come upstairs – it's quieter there."

Ralph stood transfixed as they walked towards the door, his gaze watching the huge Negro following them. With an oath he swung round and caught his sister's arm.

"By God, it's a conspiracy," he said hoarsely.

"What are you babbling about now?" Marguerite tried to free herself angrily.

"That Negro was at Rachel's house tonight. He threw me out."

"Good for him." Marguerite was unconcerned.

"You little fool!" Ralph could have choked her. "What was one of Tyler's servants doing at a trollop's house?"

"Perhaps he was one of her customers."

"Or Tyler hired her to fleece me. I met her here."

"But why should he pick on you? There are richer men in town. What reason could he have for wanting you ruined?"

"What reason indeed!" His eyes gleamed suddenly. "Did you ever see this man Babette knew?"

"No, why?" Marguerite's expression grew incredulous. "Grant and Babette – oh, no, it's too funny for words! She couldn't hold him for a moment."

"How do you know? I certainly don't."

Marguerite's gaze followed the slender figure of her sister-in-law until it disappeared around the top of the staircase. She was a child – Grant could not prefer her to a full-blooded woman, and yet the idea slowly began to possess her. If it was true, so many pieces of the puzzle would fall into place. Grant's reason for ruining Ralph – Louis working at Sans Souci – the restoration of the Big House for the woman soon to be Mrs. Tyler.

A shudder of rage ran through her. She had been discarded for a girl she had always considered cold and uninteresting. They would both pay for the insult.

"Where are you going?" Ralph demanded as she turned away.

"Your idea may not be so stupid after all. I intend to find out."

"How?"

"By finding proof of her unfaithfulness, dear brother, what else? And I know just what to look for."

An insistent knocking on the door interrupted Grant and Babette as they were taking coffee and brandy in his sitting-room. Louis had stayed only a few minutes before returning to the tables. A look of annoyance crossed his face as he said curtly,

"Who is it?"

As usual, only Sam's head appeared around the door.

"Trouble, Massa Grant. Massa Louis said be prepared."

"Damn you, man, come in and explain properly."

Cautiously Sam edged himself into the room. He had not wanted to disturb his master, but Louis St. Clair had been insistent.

"Massa Louis say you can expect you know who, about you know what, any minute." Sam scratched his head. "You know what he means?"

"The devil I can – yes, Sam – I know. Go back and tell him I'll take care of things up here."

Grant swung round on Babette and said briskly,

"Go into the bedroom and keep out of sight. I was right about Weldon – any moment he'll be up here demanding more credit."

"Does it matter if he sees me?"

"I want all the surprises to come from our side of the fence. Do as I say."

He thought she would refuse for a moment then she shrugged and went into the other room. Grant lighted a cheroot and sat down behind his desk.

He opened a bottom drawer and took out a small bundle of bills, secured with a thick rubber band. The time was ripe for a showdown.

Ralph made his entrance into the room with a boisterous, "Now – look here, Tyler. What do you mean by giving orders that no further credit is to be issued to me?"

Grant did not bat an eyelid. Weldon had been drinking again, he thought. Babette was mad to have given herself to this worthless fop. His mouth tightened.

"You are no longer welcome at Sans Souci – pay up and get out."

"I can't pay you yet, I need more time."

Ralph controlled the urge to thrust his fist into the emotionless face of the man before him. He had promised himself he would remain calm. Later, he would see his wife and persuade her to part with her sapphire pendant. "Another day, at least."

"And how will you raise enough to meet all your outstanding bills in so short a time?" Grant pushed the wad of papers he held across the desk. "A certain friend of mine was growing worried because her *ami* could not pay for the presents he had given her. I assured her she wouldn't have to give anything back. She richly deserves everything she got out of you. As you can see, everything has been paid by me. The amount still owing is shown on the top piece of paper." Grant relaxed back in his chair. "By tomorrow morning I want payment."

"It's impossible."

"A gambling debt is one of honour – even to a man like you," Grant snapped contemptuously. "If you have no money, I'll settle for your half of the St. Clair Shipping Line, plus a cash adjustment, that will keep you in women and wine for some months."

"You and that bitch, Rachel – you planned this. By God, Marguerite was right for once." Ralph spat the words across the desk, his face growing purple with rage. He hated Grant Tyler for outsmarting him – and Rachel for cheating him, but most of all he hated his sister for being so clever.

"Right about what?" Grant enquired coldly.

"You and my wife," Ralph said triumphantly. He expected a violent reaction to his words, but none came and he felt suddenly deflated. He couldn't be wrong. Grant fixed him with a piercing gaze.

"And what could your wife give me that I can't get from one of Millie's girls? You must admit they are more my type."

The words were cruel – callous, but they dispelled Ralph's confused suspicions. The idea was ludicrous; he had said so from the beginning. Babette and a gambler – ice and fire – it was stupid.

"A cash adjustment," he mumbled. "All right – I'll sign the papers in the morning."

"Tonight," Grant corrected. He produced something from his inside pocket and spread it out on the desk for Ralph to examine. "It's quite legal, I assure you. Old Montepelian drew it up earlier for me. If you'll sign it at the bottom –"

Two large bundles of notes were tossed beside the documents, together with the remainder of Ralph's I.O.U.s. "You are a fool if you don't agree. By morning I could have you banned from every house in New Orleans for not honouring a gambling debt."

Ralph called him a vile name, but he signed the paper and relinquished his hold on the Shipping Line and transferred it, together with all stocks, shares and goods to Grant Tyler.

"Now get out – I'm sick of the sight of you and so are my croupiers."

Grant rose to his feet, tucking the document back into his pocket. It had been a very satisfactory evening. Later he and Babette would celebrate at the Big House.

With hands that shook, Ralph grabbed the money from the desk.

"Don't forget the I.O.U.s," Grant said coldly as he turned to go. He sighed with relief as the door slammed behind Ralph's hurriedly departing figure.

He waited a minute, then knocked on the bedroom door.

"You can come out now. He's gone."

He returned to his desk, but when Babette did not appear – he crossed the room and flung open the door. The room was empty and the small door leading out into the corridor was half ajar. Grant swore and hurried to the top of the staircase. Ralph was making his way downstairs with what little dignity remained, but he searched the floor in vain for Babette.

CHAPTER
ELEVEN

BABETTE'S headlong flight from Sans Souci had been prompted, not so much by Ralph's presence in the next room, but by Grant's comparing her with the women on the Rue Gallatin. He had made the words sound so convincing she had covered her ears and run out into the corridor. The carriage was almost home before she had recovered her composure.

Wearily, she let herself into the house and climbed the stairs to her room. Ralph would get drunk now he had money. She had only a short while in which to pack and leave again, in case he returned unexpectedly. She would take only a small overnight case. Jemima could send the rest of her clothes to the Big House in the morning.

She stopped short in front of her bedroom. The door was open and the whole room screamed chaos. Dresses were thrown on to the bed; scattered on the floor. The bed had been stripped and her dressing-table completely ransacked.

"Missy – oh, Missy – I tried to stop her –"

Jemima looked up from the floor where she sat trying to untangle her mistress' voluminous underskirts.

"Who – ?" Babette gazed about her in bewilderment.

"Miss Marguerite. She's taken that dress. She knows. She's gone to Sans Souci to show it to Massa Ralph."

Marguerite had found her gypsy dress! Babette sank down on to the disordered bed, her eyes wide with apprehension. Grant had wanted the surprises to come from them, but now it was too late; Marguerite had beaten them to it. She would tell not only Ralph, but all the inhabitants of Sans Souci. She would not lack an audience once she began her tale of wantonness. By morning it would be common gossip and Babette would be an outcast. It had come at last – all that was left for her was to go to the Big House – to Grant Tyler.

"Pack a small valise, Jemima – I'm leaving."

The Negress stared at her in disbelief.

"Leaving – Missy B'bette. How can you, the steamer ain't going nowhere until morning – where will you go?"

"Where I belong – to Monsieur Tyler – hurry now and stop looking at me as if I've taken leave of my senses, or I won't bother to take you with me."

She jumped to her feet and paced nervously to and fro before the window while Jemima tried to find Babette's silver-backed hairbrush and comb which had been hurled across the room by an irate Marguerite.

Babette suddenly stopped her pacing and dissolved into tears.

"I can't go to him – I can't face them all – oh, Jemima, what am I to do. I'm trapped – there's only this one way out for me." Her voice trailed off and faint hope sparked in her eyes. "The riverboat – you said something about the riverboat. When does it leave?"

"On the first tide – about five o'clock."

"Why – that's only three hours from now – he wouldn't miss me, I would be free."

Free – the word hammered at her muddled brain. She clutched desperately at the unexpected chance to solve all her problems. By the time Grant discovered her absence, she would be safely away from New Orleans.

"Missy, wait – I ain't finished packing."

Jemima stretched out a detaining hand as Babette rushed past her, but it was brushed aside. By the time she reached the head of the stairs, her young mistress was already out in the street, running towards the jetty as if pursued by the devil himself.

The captain of the riverboat stared somewhat apprehensively at the dishevelled girl who presented herself before him demanding passage. It was not until she moved under the swinging arc of a deck lamp that she became familiar.

"Mrs. Weldon – why, I didn't recognise you at first. A cabin, you say? I'm sorry, but it's impossible this trip. I don't have a vacant one available."

Babette swayed back from him with a soft cry.

"But you must. It's imperative I leave New Orleans tonight."

The Captain frowned. This woman sounded hysterical. She was in no state to go anywhere.

"Believe me, Mrs. Weldon, I'd help you if I could. If there's a last-minute cancellation I'll send someone to fetch you at once –"

"I must go with you." Babette passed a hand over her eyes. Everything was swimming hazily out of focus. The huge frame of the man before her blurred and receded. She felt herself falling forward and knew no more.

A light directly above her head hurt her eyes when she opened them again. She blinked and turned her face away, muttering incoherently.

"She's coming round," a woman's voice remarked close by.

"Thank goodness, she gave me quite a turn. I suppose I ought to get in touch with Mr. Weldon, he could be worrying over her."

"I know him quite well – I've written a note. If you could find someone to deliver it for me –"

The voice trailed off. Babette opened her eyes, puzzled over the identity of this woman who knew her husband "quite well".

"You." She could hardly believe the identity of the woman who stood beside her.

Rachel leant over her, restraining hands on her shoulders as Babette struggled to sit up.

"Lie still, you're feverish. I should be sending for a doctor instead of your husband. I doubt if he'll be in any state to comfort you."

Babette felt too ill to ask how she knew that.

"Where am I?"

"My cabin – you fainted right outside it. The poor captain nearly threw a fit." Rachel perched herself on the edge of the bunk. "What are you doing on board – running away?"

"Why do you say that?" Babette tried to sound casual, but her voice trembled.

"If you were merely taking a few days' vacation, you would have booked a cabin and come on board hours ago, complete with cases. Why don't you tell me about it – I may be able to help." Rachel fixed the pillows more comfortably beneath the other girl's head and sat waiting.

Babette felt hot tears sting her eyes.

"Help! I know who you are. Why should you want to help me?"

"My association with your husband was more of a business deal than a love affair," Rachel answered truthfully, and a smile touched her crimson lips at the thought of her bank account. "Besides, I owed Grant a favour. He was only doing it for you anyway."

"Was he? Somehow I think he hasn't told you everything."

"I know he's out to ruin your husband –"

"He's out for revenge, not only on Ralph. First it was my brother, Louis – soon my turn will come. He hates us all."

"If he hates you, would he have had the Big House redecorated so lavishly?" Rachel asked. She thought of the house she might one day live in; it could never in any way compare with Grant's new palace.

"You don't know when you are well off," she added. "If my man afforded me such luxury – I'd be grateful and keep quiet."

Babette rolled her head on the pillows, trying hard to fight against crying.

"You don't understand – I shall pay a high price for my luxury. I thought marriage to Ralph was the worst ordeal – now I know different."

"Why did you marry him if you didn't love him?" Rachel said quietly.

"It was my father's wish," Babette answered. "In my family one adheres to the ways of the old country. Perhaps they are strange to you –"

"Strange and barbaric," the other said. "I wouldn't fancy being palmed off on a stranger because my daddy said so."

"There was another reason, one I cannot tell even to you. When Grant and I met and fell in love we decided to leave New Orleans and get married. Foolishly, I told Ralph and my father. Ralph threatened to expose a secret which could ruin my brother's happiness and disgrace the whole family."

"So he blackmailed you into marriage?"

Babette nodded.

"At first I thought Louis was more dear to me than Grant. He had to be, after all, he is my brother, but soon I knew I had done wrong. Ralph made me swear not to see or contact Grant before the wedding – I didn't." She shrugged. "You know the rest. He has planned and executed his revenge on each of my family in one way or another. Soon it will be complete."

"You mean when you go to live at the Big House?" Rachel asked sympathetically. Did Grant know all this, she wondered. Was he aware this girl was still pining her heart out for him?

"I shall be a prisoner in his fine mansion," Babette replied, and a tear trickled down over her ashen cheek. "How will I bear his hate – the awful contempt in his eyes when he looks at me?"

Rachel caught her slim hands and squeezed them reassuringly.

"You hurt him, Babette, and now you must face up to his revenge, but you're a lovely girl and somehow I don't think he will feel that way for long."

"Thank you. You are very kind. I wish I had known you like this before."

"Once I've found a nice little farm – you and Grant must

come to the wedding," Rachel said, and her voice was husky.
Damn Grant for hurting this child so cruelly. He needed a
good talking to.

"Face up to him, Babette, he's won, but the outcome isn't
going to be so terrible, is it? You've won too, haven't you?"

"If you look at it that way I suppose I have," Babette
answered, "but he'll never believe I still love him. That's
why I tried to run away."

"Don't force it down his throat – he's no fool – he'll realise
it if you give him half a chance. Do just as he says and let
things take their course." Rachel smiled and stood up. "Take
the advice of an expert – it won't fail." Certainly not after I've
talked with him, she thought silently.

At the sound of footsteps on the deck outside, Rachel
moved quietly from the side of the sleeping Babette, and
opened the door. Grant stood outside, his hand raised about
to knock. His gaze darted past her to the other girl, but
before he could step over the threshold she slipped out,
closing the door firmly behind her.

"I want to talk to you first."

"I'm in no mood for pleasantries," he growled.

"Don't bark at me, lover – unlike Frenchy in there, I don't
bend so easily in the wind." Rachel moved to the rail and
leaned over the side, watching a group of laughing sailors
crowded around a girl by the gangplank.

Grant hesitated, then joined her, taking a cheroot from an
inside pocket. He was angry and did not bother to hide it.

"I take it I'm about to be lectured. What lies has she fed
you?"

Rachel's anger matched his own. She had never considered
herself a woman's woman, but she recognised Babette's
defencelessness and had found herself in sympathy.

"She's in no condition to concoct any fanciful stories –
she's ill. The nearest thing to a breakdown I've ever seen,"
Rachel retorted, adding, "She's still in love with you."

In the brief flare of a match, as he lighted his cheroot,
Grant's face was bleak.

"She has been talking."

"I made her. She's quite a girl. The first I've ever known who was willing to give up the man she loved to save the family's honour. I thought that was the kind of thing you only read about in books."

"It is." Grant was loath to listen to any more. "She tried that tale with me too."

"Did you check it? Weldon blackmailed her into marrying him. He has some kind of hold over the family. Grant, for heaven's sake —"

Rachel caught his arm and jerked him around to face her when he turned towards the cabin.

"You've done her enough harm — the kid's heart is nearly broken in two."

"Monsieur Tyler does not believe I have a heart," a shaky voice said behind them.

Babette moved from the cabin doorway. They had been so engrossed, neither had realised her presence. "Your voices woke me — I heard what you said." She managed a faint smile in Rachel's direction. "It was kind of you to try, but you should know how hopeless it is." She turned to face Grant, drawing her cloak tightly around her. "I am ready to go — if you wish it."

Grant stood silent, drawing deeply on his cheroot. Even in the half-light, her pallor was alarming and he saw she clutched tightly to the door post, as if afraid without its support she might fall.

"I'll help you down to the carriage," Rachel began, but Grant put out a detaining hand.

"I can take care of her myself."

He took Babette's arm and motioned her towards the gangplank. At the head of it he hesitated and then looked back at Rachel.

"Don't forget to send me a wedding invitation," he said quietly. "Good luck, Rachel."

"Goodbye, Grant. Be fair with her."

She saw him smile.

"My set of rules is always fair – it's the others who bend them."

He paused by the waiting carriage to raise his hand in a farewell salute, then he climbed in. Rachel watched the carriage turn out of sight before returning to her cabin.

Babette sank back in her seat, her eyes closed. She did not want to make conversation and was relieved Grant did not force her to do so. Neither spoke as the carriage rolled through silent, deserted streets, past the St. Clair house, past Sans Souci where only a single light shone from one of the downstairs rooms and along the old plantation track to the Big House.

"Here we are."

Grant broke the silence at last. Her hands were ice in his as he helped her down. He frowned down at her, not wanting to feel concern, yet unable to steel himself against her pathetic countenance.

"I've had fires lighted in your apartments. I suggest you go straight to bed after you've seen Louis."

Babette's steps faltered.

"Louis is here. But why?"

"To make sure you are safe, why else?"

Grant halted before the drawing room, his expression grim.

"I've something to discuss with Sam. Louis is inside – go and put his mind at ease."

"Are you sure you can trust me alone with him? I might tell him the truth."

"Can you afford to?" Grant retorted cruelly and turned on his heel.

Louis rose from the chaise-longue as she entered and came to meet her, arms outstretched. Babette went into them willingly, glad of the unexpected comfort.

"Why have you been so long, *ma petite?* I was beginning to worry." He held her away from him, his pale eyes searching her face. "You look exhausted and you are cold. Have you caught a chill? Come and sit by the fire."

"Dear Louis, don't fuss," Babette said, but she did not protest too much and allowed him to seat her before the welcome warmth of the fire and fetch her a brandy.

"Where are your cases? I'll have them taken upstairs."

"I didn't bring any with me."

"That's a nuisance, but don't worry, I'll get them out of the house somehow. I suppose Grant rushed you out for fear Marguerite came back with Ralph."

Babette looked at him puzzledly.

"I don't understand, when did you see her?"

"Tonight, of course. Don't tell me Grant hasn't enlightened you."

"I only know Marguerite ransacked my room and found the gypsy dress. Jemima said she went to Sans Souci to find Ralph."

"She didn't find him. She found Grant and myself instead. The dress has been burnt. I entertained her while Grant came to fetch you. We wanted you safely here before she reached Ralph."

"That was sweet of you." Babette put aside her empty glass and leaned back in her chair with a sigh. "By now, he will know everything and by tomorrow —" She broke off, her eyes flooding with tears.

"Let tomorrow take care of itself," Louis answered gently. He bent over her and lightly kissed her forehead. "I'm a big boy now. I'll take care of myself from now on, and Grant will look after you."

"Babette has never doubted that for a moment," Grant said, coming through the door behind him.

Louis threw him a swift look, sensing a deeper meaning behind the words, but the other man's expression betrayed nothing and he dismissed his suspicions.

"I was just telling Babette how we took care of Marguerite," he said.

Grant poured himself a drink and replenished Babette's

glass despite her protest. With a smile he pressed it into her hand.

"Drink it and then go to bed."

"I'll arrange to get Babette's cases here tomorrow," Louis said.

"There's no need. I've already made the necessary arrangements with Sam and Jemima," Grant answered. "You would like your own maid here, of course?" he asked Babette.

"If possible. Ralph and Marguerite will make her life unbearable otherwise. They might even get rid of her."

Louis swallowed the last of his whisky with a grimace.

"It's time I left you two in peace."

"You are not going home?" Babette asked, worriedly. She tried to sit upright, but her limbs felt suddenly weak and she sank back blinking tiredly. "Louis, no – Ralph –"

"I must go back to find out what those two are up to, for all our sakes."

He looked up at Grant. "If it's all right with you, I'll move into Sans Souci some time tomorrow."

"Any time," Grant replied amiably. "Make yourself at home, you know your way around by now. I'll be over around seven in the evening."

"Then I'll say goodnight until tomorrow." Louis said. He leaned over Babette only to find her eyes tightly closed.

"She's fallen asleep – *pauvre petite.*"

"She'll sleep solidly for at least twelve hours." Grant gently removed the empty glass from her lax fingers. "Her drink was laced with the strongest sleeping draught I could find."

"She will need all her strength to face our so-called Society," Louis said slowly, "Don't let them hurt her too much."

"They won't even reach her," Grant assured him, and he meant it.

"You will have your work cut out when Ralph starts talking," Louis said.

"Don't you think it's time you told me this grisly secret of

yours," Grant murmured. "If I'm to protect Babette, I need
to know what cards my opponent holds."

Louis nodded.

"You are right, of course." His fingers touched his sister's
tousled hair. "*Pauvre* Babette – she has sacrificed so much
for me." He sighed, his eyes filling with pain as memories
came flooding back. "Five years ago I met a girl. She came
from the other side of town. Had I set her up in a little place of
her own and visited her discreetly, my father would have said
nothing, but I wanted to marry her, despite the unforgivable
fact that she was Creole."

Grant said nothing. Louis smiled.

"I do not shock you, but then you are a man of the world
and your background is so different to mine. You cannot
imagine the prejudices we would have had to face."

"There are other places."

Louis nodded.

"We thought of that. We were married in secret and I
found a little house for her overlooking the river until I had
enough money to get us both away. Babette was wonderful.
She visited Ginette often – they became great friends."

Louis broke off to light a cigar. Grant saw his hands were
trembling. "My father suddenly decided to send me away on
business. I had no idea he had found out I was still seeing
Ginette. While I was away he followed Babette to the house
and waited until she left, then went in. *Mon dieu*, the things
he said to her – he drove her out of her mind." He looked up
at Grant, pale and trembling.

"She carried my child. My father told her the marriage was
not valid, that the priest who married us was really one of my
friends and the whole thing was a fake. He said I had gone
away, in case she tried to say the child was mine. He gave her
money and told her to buy herself a husband if she was
worried about her good name. After he had gone Ginette
wrote me a letter and told me exactly what he had said, and
then she drowned herself.

"Babette was ill for weeks. She blamed herself for being

careless and allowing father to follow her. That's why she married Weldon – to spare me further pain. She swore she would never allow people to despoil those few short months Ginette and I had together and I allowed her to do it. I should have killed that man long ago. My only consolation is that he has never had the pleasure of touching her."

"Are you telling me she's his wife in name only?" Grant demanded roughly. Babette's pale face swam before his tortured vision. Only now did he understand how completely he had been blinded by jealousy.

"My sister has never belonged to any man except you, my friend – and she has never loved anyone else. She did what she did out of love for me and in those days I was too weak to refuse such a self-sacrifice on her part. My marriage to Ginette was no farce and I have many happy memories. Seeing you and Babette has made me realise a few months were better than none at all." He smiled and moved towards the door. "I am of a mind to see Ralph and settle our differences once and for all. Babette must not be made to pay for my mistakes. My blessings on you both. Be happy."

The slam of the front door roused Grant from a shocked stupor. Babette stirred faintly as he lifted her up in his arms, but did not awaken, nor as he laid her on the bed in the pale blue bedroom, beneath the watchful gaze of the two golden cherubs and drew the silk covers over her. For a long while he remained at her side, staring down at the lovely face, so peaceful and relaxed in sleep. Then silently he crossed the thickly carpeted floor and went into his own rooms. He knew now there was only one course of action left open to him.

At about the same time as Grant was escorting Babette to the Big House, Marguerite was acquainting her brother with all the elaborated facts of his wife's unfaithfulness. Her bitter, scorching words maddened his already drink-sodden mind and sent him stumbling blindly out of the house and into the nearest tavern. Marguerite's revenge was well on its way to being complete. The ugly seeds she had sown would multiply with the addition of raw liquor. By the time the gossips got hold of the story, it would have been distorted out of all proportion. Grant Tyler and Babette would be lucky to get out of town without being tarred and feathered.

Babette awoke to a bedroom bathed in late afternoon sunshine. She lay still, dazed with sleep, until gradually as her eyes roved about the room, she became aware of her surroundings and of what had passed the previous evening.

The hands on the tiny Louis XVI clock on the table beside her showed four o'clock. She had almost slept through a whole day. Her first thoughts were of Louis. Where was he? At Sans Souci perhaps – or downstairs, waiting for her to awake?

Pushing aside the coverlet, she stood up and tugged on the bell-rope beside the bed. While she waited for someone to come, she wandered around the room, discovering that all her dresses had been neatly hung in the huge ornate wardrobe. The dresser too, was full and her toilet requisites were laid out on the dressing-table. Someone had been very busy indeed.

She could not suppress a cry of delight as Jemima's coalblack features appeared around the doorway.

"Jemima – when did you arrive? Did you bring my things?"

"Monsieur Tyler sent Sam to collect me early this morning before anyone was awake. We sneaked out real sly – lordy, but I'd like to hear what they're saying now."

"I don't think I would," Babette returned. "Where is Monsieur Tyler?"

"Downstairs in his study – he has given instructions dinner is to be served up here in your apartments."

Babette bit her lips. He was making it painfully obvious he intended to be master of the situation from the very beginning.

"Very well, Jemima. Prepare my bath and lay out an evening gown – the green satin, I think."

A clock somewhere in the house was striking eight o'clock

as Babette descended the stairs to the study determined to hold her own against Grant at all costs. She was not white trash to be kept upstairs out of sight and used for his pleasure when and where he demanded. She had wronged him, but his revenge had been far more terrible than any hurt she had inflicted. She knocked twice on the oak panelled door. There was no answer. Quietly she turned the handle and went into the room.

In a high-backed chair before the fire Grant sprawled sleeping soundly. His hair was tousled – he wore no jacket and his white shirt was open at the neck. A black silk tie was thrown on the table beside a bottle of whisky and an empty glass. As she moved nearer, the aroma of whisky grew stronger. He had obviously been drinking for some considerable time.

The writing desk against the far wall was open and papers were littered across the top. Curiously, Babette stepped quietly past the sleeping figure to examine them. The deeds to the St. Clair house were there and a half-finished letter. He must have been writing it before he fell asleep. Babette did not stop to consider the rights and wrongs of her prying, for she had seen that a nearby envelope was addressed to her. Her hand trembled as she picked up the letter.

"My petite Babette:

When you read these words I shall no longer be in New Orleans. I am leaving tonight while you are asleep. Tomorrow, you will be free of me. Tonight, I learned of the great wrong I have done you from Louis, and I would gladly give my life to be able to turn back the clock and be with you once again beside the bayou. Words are meaningless at a time like this and I cannot be sure you will believe me, that is why I am going away. This house is yours and you will find I have also left you the deeds to your old home. It is only right you should go back there, if you wish. Half of all the money from the gambling tables of Sans Souci will be paid into my bank in your name. Do not refuse it. I must know you are free of Ralph Weldon and this is the only way. You will never see me again, but I shall not forget the girl I once called 'Blue-eyes' –"

Babette was only just able to read the last two lines, for they had been deleted with several strokes of the pen. Tears blurred her vision and she swayed forward, clutching at the bureau for support. The letter was plucked from her nerveless fingers and a heavy hand laid on her arm, pulling her about.

"Have you finished reading my private correspondence?" Grant demanded dryly.

"It – it was written to me," Babette stammered.

"You were not meant to see it until tomorrow." Grant cursed himself for falling asleep. He had drunk too much; glass after glass while he tried to finish the letter. White-faced, he stared down into her stricken features, then with something near to a groan, he wheeled away from her, throwing the crumpled letter into the fire.

"Don't go – I love you." The words broke from Babette's lips in a rush. "You know the truth now, there is no need for us to go on hurting each other."

"I must go. It will be better for both of us." It was a long while before he had enough composure to turn and look at her again. God! She looked lovelier tonight than ever before. His hands clenched into tight fists at his side.

"If you go, then I'll follow you. I have no pride left, Grant – only my love. Somehow I will make you believe me. Without you I shall die, I know it." Babette stepped closer to him, her face upturned to his, tear-streaked, appealing. "Let me stay with you – please – please let me stay –"

Grant's eyes grew dark. One hand touched her wet cheek and the next moment she was in his arms. The room swam about her – her senses reeled under the fierceness of his kisses. With the first touch of his lips on hers, all suspicions – jealousy – all thoughts of revenge and bitterness disappeared. Grant held his "Blue-eyes" in his arms – the girl he had fallen in love with beside the bayou and tried so hard to destroy. Babette felt faint with happiness.

A long while later, seated close together on the couch in the drawing room, Grant allowed her to draw away from him long enough to smooth some order into her dishevelled hair.

"Ralph won't set me free," Babette whispered. She avoided the arm he tried to slip about her shoulders, knowing there must come a time when they had to talk about the future. "I know he won't. He'll cover my absence by telling everyone I've gone to stay with friends in Baton Rouge for an indefinite period. Everyone will believe him, they have no reason not to. He may even make the odd trip up river pretending to visit me." She shook her head sadly, "No, *mon ami* – he will never set me free – only his death will do that."

Grant's eyes narrowed sharply. That way out he had not contemplated. Babette looked at him sudden alarm springing to her eyes.

"No – you must not harm him. We will go away, as you said, it doesn't matter as long as we are together."

"If I wanted you only as my mistress, I would have taken you long ago," Grant said fiercely. "I want you to be my wife."

"I want us to be together always, it doesn't matter how. I'd rather be your mistress than not be with you at all. Don't you understand?" Babette pleaded.

"*Je t'adore –je t'aime,*" Grant murmured in the soft Creole French he reserved for occasions when they were alone together. He bent to kiss her eager lips and her nearness made his body ache with the desire to possess her. "We will do as you wish, but I swear one day you will wear my ring and bear my name."

"Mrs. Grant Tyler," Babette laughed softly. "It has such a wonderful sound."

She laid her head against his shoulder with a sigh, feeling suddenly drained of all strength. In a while they would go upstairs and he would make love to her. She would belong to him as she had never belonged to Ralph, her husband, or any

other man. It would be the fulfilment of the long months of
waiting – dreaming.

"When shall we leave?" she asked softly.

"As soon as I've arranged matters here," Grant answered.
"It will be easier now Louis is taking over Sans Souci."

"Do you really mean him to run it for you?"

"Of course – he's proved he is capable –"

"And the Big House?" There was a wistful note in
Babette's voice. "I'm almost sad to leave it after the way
you've had it arranged. Had things been different I could
have been happy here."

"We'll find another place. I'll have this one put up for sale.
Decide what furniture and other items you want to keep and
they can be stored until we send for them." Grant broke off,
his eyes searching her face as if for some sign of indecision.
He saw none, yet he found himself asking, "Are you sure, my
darling? Are you really sure?"

Babette nodded slowly.

"Yes, Grant, I am sure."

The fire on the waterfront broke out without warning and
within minutes was consuming the entire offices of the St.
Clair Shipping Line and creeping steadily, relentlessly,
towards warehouses packed to capacity with valuable cargoes
awaiting shipment.

When Grant and Babette arrived the heat was so intense
that no one could get near to any of the buildings.

"It looks bad. There's nothing you can do here, *m'amie*.
Go back to the house," Grant said, climbing down from the
carriage.

Babette shook her head.

"I'll wait. Can you see Louis? I heard one of your clerks say
he was here."

"I'll try and find him. If I do, I'll send him back to stay
with you." Grant stared at the flames with a sardonic twist to
his mouth. "Oh well – I was never meant to have everything," he muttered dryly.

Louis St. Clair was not among the crowd of spectators. From his chief clerk Grant heard how Louis and Ralph Weldon were seen arguing on the quayside. They had gone into one of the warehouses and not long afterwards the fire had broken out. Grant knew there was no way of knowing if it was an accident or a deliberate act.

"I am of a mind to see Ralph and settle our differences once and for all." The significance of Louis' words came back to him with horrifying clarity. He started towards the blazing warehouses, shaking off restraining hands, knowing it was too late – yet unable to stand by and do nothing.

The intense heat drove him back. He yelled Louis' name, but above the roar of the inferno of flames his voice was little more than a whisper.

A sheet of flame shot skywards and hot embers showered him, burning his clothes as he threw his hands up to protect his face. When he lowered them, there was nothing left of the warehouses but a mass of blazing rubble.

Late the following morning while Babette still slept under heavy sedation, a police officer brought news of the recovery of the bodies. Grant talked alone with him in the study.

"They found Mr. Louis' body not far from Mr. Weldon's," the man said in a sympathetic voice. "It looks as if he was trying to reach him when the roof cllapsed. Poor Mrs. Weldon, husband and brother both lost."

Grant agreed, but for days afterwards while Babette lay feverishly ill in her bed, he had time to wonder.

Something told him Louis had not been making idle threats the last time they were together. He had not been attempting to reach his hated brother-in-law, as everyone believed, but had prevented his escape, prepared to sacrifice his life for his sister's happiness.

He never told Babette his suspicions, or her brother's last remarks, when she grew well and strong again. Both bodies had been found, that was all he deemed it necessary to tell her. Perhaps in the years ahead, a time would come when they could talk about what had happened, without the memories proving too painful.

Three months later, on a glorious summer day, they were married in the tiny church of St. Joseph's near Sans Souci. Ralph's death had made it possible for them both to stay in New Orleans and live out their lives at the Big House as if the unfortunate marriage had never taken place. As the boat taking them on their honeymoon moved away from the quay, Babette looked up at Grant, suddenly apprehensive.

"Grant – do you think Louis approves this time?" she asked hesitantly.

"He wanted us to be together one day," Grant replied quietly, and the smile returned to her face. "In fact, I think he planned it all along," he added and silently offered grateful thanks to their absent benefactor.

AVAILABLE THIS MONTH

THE DAMASK ROSE
by Polly Meyrick

From a menial position as a governess in
Lancashire, Isabelle Harrowby is miraculously
rescued from drudgery by her wealthy Uncle
Joshua, who brings her to London. Far too
tall and believing herself plain, Isabelle's
chances of finding a dashing Regency buck
appear to be slim — until the suave Marquis
of Dale is mesmerized by her violet eyes. His
attention is sufficient to launch Isabelle on
London society, but any hopes she secretly
entertains of capturing the noble lord are
dashed when she learns of his secret engagement to the worldly Caroline Barford.

**October's other memorable Historical novel of
romance, intrigue and excitement — order your
copy today!**

Old-fashioned value at 60p net

Masquerade
HISTORICAL ROMANCES

ANNOUNCING

Masquerade
NOVEMBER TITLES

JOANNA
Patricia Ormsby

Irrepressible Joanna and her cousin Mollie, in
London for the Season, quickly attract the
attention of the most eligible suitors. All goes
well until the arrival of Joanna's rejected suitor,
Lord Inchman, who threatens to kill any rivals.
Confusion increases when her friend Barbara's
admirer decides to settle the question of
Joanna's hand in marriage with a duel.

THE QUEEN'S CAPTAIN
Margaret Hope

Beth Howard refuses to enter into marriage with
a man who has not even bothered to meet her
— the mighty Captain Danyell. When she runs
away from home instead, she is set upon by a.
press gang and forced to serve as cabin 'boy' in
Queen Elizabeth's navy. Imagine her horror on
finding that her Captain is James Danyell — the
one man she is trying to avoid . . .

Old-fashioned value at 60p net

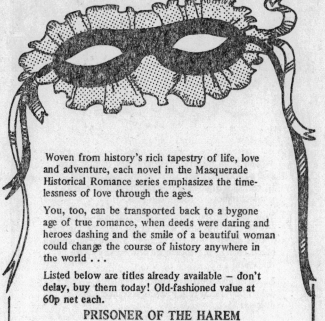

Woven from history's rich tapestry of life, love and adventure, each novel in the Masquerade Historical Romance series emphasizes the timelessness of love through the ages.

You, too, can be transported back to a bygone age of true romance, when deeds were daring and heroes dashing and the smile of a beautiful woman could change the course of history anywhere in the world . . .

Listed below are titles already available – don't delay, buy them today! Old-fashioned value at 60p net each.

PRISONER OF THE HAREM
by Julia Herbert

It is Naples in 1793. Felicity thinks nothing could be worse for her heiress cousin Rosanna than elopement with a Neapolitan artist, but ahead of the two girls lies abduction by Barbary pirates and imprisonment in a harem in Algiers. Apart from ransom, their only source of rescue might be a handsome soldier they dare not trust.

LADY OF DARKNESS
by Lisa Montague

Serena Apsley's secret mission is almost foiled by England's enemies and her failure to meet her contact. Instead she is threatened by the dangerous yet fascinating highwayman called Darkness who interferes with her plans and silences her protests with kisses.

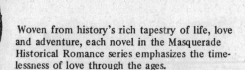

Woven from history's rich tapestry of life, love and adventure, each novel in the Masquerade Historical Romance series emphasizes the time-lessness of love through the ages.

You, too, can be transported back to a bygone age of true romance, when deeds were daring and heroes dashing and the smile of a beautiful woman could change the course of history anywhere in the world ...

Listed below are titles already available — don't delay, buy them today! Old-fashioned value at 60p net each.

THE LAIRD'S FRENCH BRIDE
by Judith Stewart

'Sold' into a loveless marriage in payment for a debt of gratitude, Catherine du Plas leaves Normandy to live in Michael MacGregor's remote Scottish castle. Her husband's passionate demands force her to return to France, the dangers of the Revolution and her childhood sweetheart.

Realising how much he needs Catherine, Michael arrives in time to save her from the revolutionary mob.

THE NOTORIOUS LADY MAY
by Julia Murray

Wounded in the Peninsular War, Captain Harbury returns to England to have a brief but tempestuous encounter with the headstrong Lady Corinna. He becomes fascinated when she is mistakenly pointed out as the notorious Lady May, the most scandalous woman in Regency society. Lady Corinna maintains the deception until Captain Harbury is challenged by the true Lady May's admirer.